Union
Writes

Writing on the Wall
Toxteth Library
Windsor Street, Liverpool
L8 1XF

Published by Writing on the Wall 2019
© Remains with Authors

Cover Design by Katrina Paterson
Layout by Daniel Turner
ISBN: 978-1-910580-39-4

0151 703 0020
info@writingonthewall.org.uk
www.writingonthewall.org.uk

Contents

Foreword

At Writing on the Wall, we understand the enormous value of providing pathways for working-class and underrepresented writers to gain access to the writing industry. Writing shouldn't be an aspirational or unlikely idea – it's one of the best ways we can engage with ourselves and those around us. Through our courses, we want to make writing accessible and attainable for everyone who wants to do it.

Recent commentary about writers of shows such as Fleabag, written by Phoebe Waller-Bridge, have brought class and privilege to the forefront of conversation about writers and access to such careers. The show's frank and humorous exploration of vulnerability, family and modern-day life is something most of us can relate to, but it's a fair point to consider how many of us could actually be afforded the opportunity, and indeed the time, to write about it in the way Waller-Bridge has managed. It's so important to provide writing opportunities for people without the privilege of networks and private education. Without these pathways there would be no representation within the arts. The impact of this is a lack of education for everyone about diverse experiences and outlooks. Write for Work does exactly that and we are immensely proud of the work created in the book.

We are privileged to be continuing our successful partnership with Unite the Union on this innovative project and we'd like to thank them, with a special mention to Keith Lewis (Unite Construction Union Learning Fund Manager) for his continued advocacy of the project. A special thank you belongs to The North West TUC, particularly Lynn Collins, for championing this project from the beginning and to our staff team at WoW for their continued dedication and hard work.

It takes an incredible amount of commitment and dedication to produce work of such high calibre but it also takes a certain amount of vulnerability to share it. We would like to congratulate all the participants on the course for the outstanding work they've produced. We hope you enjoy reading the anthology and make sure to share it with friends, family and colleagues.

Madeline Heneghan & Mike Morris
Writing on the Wall Co-Directors

Introduction

Unions are a collective, a coming together of people who share a common goal, whether to advocate for our rights or to share in our stories. Working with Unite the Union on our second instalment of the Write for Work project, we were able to expand upon a shared vision of this innovative project. Writer's developed their skillset and growth within the workplace and beyond and emphasised that sense of solidarity which only comes from sharing and listening to our stories.

The often precarious nature of the employment industry, especially the writing sector, is one that's always transforming. Write for Work has established an exciting pathway into a difficult landscape. With the fast-paced changes in the writing sector it's hard to ignore the rise of online media and our vast consumption of this, whether it be listening to podcasts, reading blogs, spoken word artists engaging social commentary on today's society, and the gaming industry becoming one of the leading employers within the writing sector. One thing is abundantly clear: being able to write and write well is imperative within most sectors.

This programme takes a holistic approach, allowing participants to see into the varied journeys and experiences of professional writers, offering diverse experiences of how to break into the industry. Over the course of ten weeks the participants worked with ten writers and industry professionals who delivered inspiring workshops in their areas of expertise. I would like to take this opportunity to thank all the writers who delivered. They fostered a positive, encouraging environment, and imparted invaluable knowledge.

Thank you to The Radisson Blu Hotel, Unite the Union, and a special mention to Keith Lewis for his support. I would also like to thank the WoW team who work tirelessly to make sure projects like these come to fruition, but most importantly I would like to thank the participants. Keep on telling your stories!

Lauren Buxton
Project Worker
Writing on the Wall

Preface

On behalf of Learn with Unite, I am delighted to be given the opportunity to introduce what is the second course and publication Unite the Union has been able to support through the Union Learning Fund (ULF). This Write for Work course was offered to ULF project staff and writers within the community who had expressed an interest in participating in this Writing on the Wall initiative.

After the previous success and publication of Writers Unite! the second instalment was based on the same approach and principles underpinning our previous project and delivery. The belief that trade unions such as Unite have a role in supporting learners to express themselves through writing, and enjoy doing it, is an essential ambition of the Learn with Unite ULF project. Promoting reading and writing skills are key to the role of ULF project workers and learning organisers.

This is ground-breaking activity for Learn with Unite and contributes to the objective of Unite the Union to reach out beyond the workplace and support both members and activists in local communities. The dynamic and polarised political landscape we find ourselves in, it has never been more important for workers and members of our different communities to find their voice and express their opinions through writing. Social media and access to information has created opportunities for individuals to develop a broader narrative. Alternatively, the ability to tell a story and enjoy writing is fundamental to the objectives of this initiative.

This Write for Work course covered a diverse range of subjects and was delivered by specialists and mentors in their respective fields. Topics included blogging, pod-casting, copywriting, editing, journalism and reportage. We made changes to the delivery of the course with it being presented over a shorter timeline than previously and incorporating two residential weekends. Feedback suggests these changes were successful with a near 100% retention rate of students and the creation of an environment where learners and mentors exchanged work and supported each other through what is often the stressful journey of producing written work for publication.

It is essential to thank the people and organisations who helped facilitate this unique piece of work. Writing on the Wall is an initiative and company that Unite is proud to be associated with. Particular thanks go to Emma and Lauren for all their hard work in facilitating the course; the North West TUC for instigating this work at the very beginning; and the ULF team based in Liverpool who supported this initiative from its initiation. Their help with organising the residentials and administration was key. Finally, and most importantly, huge thanks to the students for their commitment, their contributions and their written work submitted for publication.

I hope you enjoy the stories and contributions from all participants, and you are able to recognise from the writing, the passion and talent nurtured and developed as a result of this stimulating and motivating course.

Keith Lewis
Learn with Unite Construction Union
Learning Fund Manager

Brexit, Brexit, Brexit
Debra Chisango

I embraced you when I first heard of you
You were beautifully wrapped
You made so much sense when you were advertised
The £350 million a week saving caught my heart and soul
I felt the EU was not fair, and finally thought something
good was happening
The NHS was on a downfall but now it would
become better.

It took two-and-half years to unwrap you
And find out who you really are
Your unfolding has given me so much confusion
The whole world is confused too
My friends and family cannot understand
You have become the longest present I have ever known
to unwrap.

You have become such a menace like Dennis the Menace
The PM has gone back and forward to Brussels more
than any other
Hoping to turn you around for the best
But your impact is too much
The Irish backstop would have stopped you
Yet this did not phase you and you still pressed on.

All I wake up to is your name
You are the talk of every meal, breakfast, lunch and tea
Someone thought you were the new name of a cereal

I hope at this stage you are also thinking about a U-turn
I feel like we are faced with the dilemma of Deal or
No Deal
Thought *Deal or No Deal* was a TV show but with you
it's reality.

Not everyone has the knowledge of World War 1 and 2
Compared to the knowledge they have of you
I am confident there will be a child named after you
That you will never be forgotten
History will be written about you and
the curriculum changed
History lessons will have you included.

Brexit please bring an understanding before it's too late
Now I need to apply for a visa
To go in search of the sun
The ones that supported you are confused too
They are watching the havoc you are causing from
the terraces
The parliament is divided.

All we talk about is you BREXIT
Even the children want to know you
Your days are numbered and we're hopeful for the best.
29 March was your final day
But you decided this was not for you
And we continue counting the cost.

Susan
Nicki McCubbing

'Super match Game, Super match Game'... that was the jingle from *Blankety Blank*, a quiz show she watched as a kid. Every now and then she'd say the words out loud without meaning to, like after she'd given directions to a stranger or when she ate a Malteser. Super match Game was the bit in the show when the game got serious. I heard her say it once when she sat down on the toilet in the cubicle next to me in the pub. She farted and then sang, 'Super match Game' after it, quietly. She didn't know I was next door to her. These were the things I loved about Susan.

I didn't know why I was meeting up with her at the time, other than that I wanted to be dead for a while. I wanted to be like Susan. I admired her resilience, how she was a bit invisible; not a looker, nothing that stood out until you actually looked and then you noticed everything. She reminded me of a sparrow that's the same colour as the floor. She was getting by. Her life was fucked but she still bought plants. In those few months of knowing her I never ever told anyone I was meeting Susan and when I stopped meeting up with her, I felt relieved. It was my very boring version of running away and living on the streets. No drugs or prostitution – just drinking wine in secret bars with a middle-aged woman who sometimes wore a chain belt.

When I met her, I was twenty-five and Susan was forty-eight. She was petite with very boring short brown hair. Her clothes were dull, and her perfume was heavy. Susan's face looked slightly appalled and a bit dirty like she should either scrub it or put make up over it - but chose neither. I had my hair in two plaits pinned to my head like Heidi and was wearing all black to look thinner, preferably invisible. My shoes were brown and overblown sensible like the type the Mr Men wore. We met at a social event called 'Meet It'. It wasn't a club to meet a romantic other - it was a place to make friends. I didn't need new friends, but I wanted new friends. There were about nine women there who needed new friends and two men who needed a shag. I thought about shagging one of them even though he was in his sixties and desperate in every way. I thought it might make him feel lucky for once.

Susan had been going to 'Meet It' longer than me. She told me she'd already met a woman two weeks earlier and they'd joked about being there at all. Like everyone did. None of us were the type to be there usually but of course we were all there. Susan and this new friend had arranged to go out for a glass of wine. She said she felt a bit ridiculous but also a bit excited. I think she liked the awkwardness of it. They met in a theatre bar. It was empty because everybody was inside watching the show. It had started off well with lots of jokes about their lives but after a few drinks they started to talk about their exes. Susan got quite angry about hers and so did the woman. Despite the fact they'd laughed and been open during their meeting, Susan went home on the bus with a sense of dread. The next day the woman sent Susan a message saying, 'I don't want to meet up with you again.' Susan asked her why and the woman replied, 'You're too negative.' Susan had responded, 'Thank you.' She was grateful for somebody telling her the truth. The woman never went back to 'Meet It', but Susan did.

Susan was unemployed like me. She was back living with her parents after losing the 'Big Three - house, partner, and job', twice in the last seven years. I thought this was unbelievable but still did not question her. Her older sister was also living in her parent's house as she too was going through a divorce. There was a lot of late-night crying in nightgowns and cruel home truths going back to their teens. Their mum had just bought a Bee Gees Live CD so every evening they ate their meal to *'You Should be Dancing'* live in Las Vegas as that was the first song on the album. Living there was hell, but they all grew to love the familiarity and the order of the songs on that CD. I felt sorry for her parents having their middle-aged daughters back at home, but I guessed they were probably to blame somehow.

I was also back living with my parents. I'd recently walked away from my job and my boyfriend of five years. We were engaged and the wedding was two months away. I'd realised I didn't want to marry him. He didn't make me happy. I hated all of his jeans and how he spoke on the phone to other people. Sometimes I would grab his dirty undies and smell them to hate him even more. It wasn't the life I wanted.

I was in the process of cancelling everything to do with the wedding. My friends and family looked at me differently now. They'd arranged my hen night and had planned how the whole thing would pan out on social media. Their fake smiles were loaded with disappointment and fear. It made me hate spending time with them. I'd noticed they'd stopped liking the sarcastic memes I was putting on Instagram and my input into our group chats was getting ignored too. I had a feeling there were other separate group chats and the subject was me. I didn't want to be around people who loved me or knew me. That's why I was at 'Meet It'. I was going to be the real me. Not cool. I wasn't going to laugh much. I was going to wear comfortable clothes. Fuck it, I was going to get a waterproof coat and it was going to be navy blue. What was the point in getting wet anymore?

When Susan and I started talking at 'Meet It' there was a feeling of relief. Neither of us had to try hard. She had looked at me and said, 'Is there somebody in here wearing patchouli oil?' I laughed and said, 'Yes that's me. I found an old bottle of it my old stuff at my mum's and decided to wear it tonight for some reason. I think it's actually off.' Susan laughed back and said, 'It's hard to tell if something is off if it's meant to smell like old mould anyway.' She was quietly spoken with a soft northern accent and her breath smelt like breadsticks and tea. She told me she used to wear patchouli oil in the 90s when she was into Heavy Metal. She didn't look like she'd ever been into Heavy Metal, not even a sneaky gothic ring or anything. I remember a stranger asked her where the nearest cashpoint was, and she pointed and afterwards said, 'Super match Game' under her breath but I heard her. It felt like a sign that only I could hear her.

I knew she was the one I was meant to meet at 'Meet It' because it was the morning I'd decided to not be cool anymore. It was like when I was at school and I stopped buying a cool version of my uniform and just bought the basic, plain one. No more sneaky patterns on the shirts or tight jumpers or short skirts. It was just a uniform. I was fourteen and I'd given up. This was the second time I was giving up. I don't think Susan had ever given up, but she wasn't trying either.

Susan and I exchanged numbers and arranged to go out drinking nearly straight away. The first time we went out it was to a bikers' pub. I wore my waterproof jacket. I saw this as an act of rebellion. The new me. Susan wore a velvet jacket and her chain belt. The bar had red lighting and a huge smashed framed picture of Marilyn Monroe on the wall next to a large photo of Karl Marx. We sat on uncomfortable wooden benches which made it hard to slump later on. We started off talking about music and then after a few drinks it turned to men. She told me about her exes and got angry about the financial implications of splitting up. I told her about leaving my boyfriend when I was about to get married. She didn't really say anything about that, and I thought she would.

It didn't matter to Susan who I was or what I did. I went to tell her once that I'd done a marathon for charity and that I could play the violin, but she wasn't interested. I'm surprised she even knew my name. It wasn't that she was self-centred; it was more that she was trying to deal with her own life. It was a mess. She was living in a state of dull terror. No future. No kids. I don't think she wanted kids or even really liked them – she just worried about being an old woman with no kids. Susan told me she had two nephews from her younger sister (the normal one of the three sisters). They were aged eight and six. She sometimes took them to the museum or to see a film that she wanted to see. Despite the fact they were nice enough, Susan fucking hated those kids. She hated the fabric of the football kits they wore, the faint smell of piss on their hands, their school photos and their hopes for the future. She hated how everyone had to pretend around them and act like they were interested in their school reports or how good they were at swimming. It was embarrassing for everyone.

Susan resented how much time her own parents had to spend with these kids, their grandkids. When they were there, she found herself fantasizing about bending their fingers back until they snapped or telling them that it was better before they were born. She wished they'd fuck off so they could talk like adults about real things like divorce and how it's impossible to get a job. She told me this one night when she was drunk. I'd laughed but Susan only smiled back. She then looked down and squeezed her thumb three times.

Eventually we began to go out drinking more regularly, mainly to rough rock bars that smelt like owls and real ale and bleach at the beginning of the night. The music was always loud, and we had to sit close to one another to hear the conversation. We began to drink more and more each time we went out. We spoke about people in our lives that we knew the other person would never meet. One night I told her about my friend who had stopped contacting me since I left my boyfriend. I'd tagged her in a photo of a guinea pig on Instagram that I thought she would love but she never responded, even though I could see she'd commented on other people's photos that same day. I cried and said, 'She shouldn't be writing on other people's stuff if she hasn't got the courtesy to reply to me. It's just rude.' Susan didn't have Instagram, but she looked at me like she was sorry.

On some nights Susan would cry a bit when she spoke about not being able to find a job. One week she'd been for an interview to work in a call centre but had walked out when they'd asked her how she'd react to angry customers. Susan previously had a good job in marketing and said she was better at selling things than selling herself. I rarely spoke about how I felt. I wasn't really there anyway. The old me was about to be married and was going on her hen weekend with her old mates. This new me was meeting up with this woman with short hair that stuck out at the nape of her neck. I always wanted to get those bits of hair in my fingers and cut it off with scissors. Sometimes Susan would get angry about her sisters and I used to say the same thing over and over to her, 'It's not your fault. Life is just shit. Fuck them all.' A few times we held hands under the table while Iron Maiden or Motorhead played on the juke box. She squeezed my thumb and I knew she understood how I felt about everything without having ever really told her any of it.

One night we met outside the usual pub at seven and we went inside. Susan seemed agitated. She was annoyed about her bus being late and the weather and how a kid had been saying 'crab's eyes' over and over on the bus to his grandad. It was the first time I'd seen her like this. An older man looked at us in the way we'd grown accustomed in these bars - wondering what our situation was and how it could be used to briefly turn him on. Were we lesbians? A mother and daughter? Work colleagues? He needed to know, so we could fulfil a service like a picture on the back of the jigsaw box. She was repeatedly tapping her metal key ring (of an angel with a crystal inside the heart) hard on the bar. 'Hello ladies,' he said. 'What have we got here?' I smiled politely and tried to catch the eye of the barman to order our drinks. Susan was not in the mood for this guy tonight. 'What do you mean 'What have we got here?' You fucking prick!' Our drinks were on the bar now. Motley Crue were playing on the juke box. I wished I was on my hen night sucking cocktails through plastic dicks. I looked at Susan. I knew what was coming. I'd seen this before in bars, only this time I was with the star of the show not just witnessing it. The man stepped back. 'Just being friendly,' he said, and he moved back to the wall. He looked embarrassed. Susan didn't look away from him though. She was breathing differently. I think she'd forgotten the aim of being here was to drink a drink. She was like a wrestler filming her promo video except she wasn't wearing a cape; she was wearing a statement necklace and work clothes from Matalan and she didn't even have a job. She was the shittiest wrestler ever but also the best one that had ever lived.

'You think we shouldn't be in here? You think you can make us feel like that in a pub?' she said to him.

'Alright, love, I wasn't even looking at you. It was the other one. Don't flatter yourself,' he said avoiding her eyes by looking at the smashed picture of Marilyn Monroe.

We all knew in that bar at that moment the game was getting serious but none of us knew how to fill the void with the correct answer to win. Susan walked over to him, went right up close and spat in his bewildered, pathetic face.

Before she could do more, the barman had hold of her and was throwing her out onto the street. She was kicking and sort of crying and screaming and laughing all at once. The barman said to me, 'You'd better get her home! Get her in a cab and get her home!' I didn't know where she lived. I didn't even know her surname and her chain belt had broken. I'm not sure if Susan had been drinking before she'd met me, but she was sat on the curb saying, 'Tell me why I don't like Mondays, tell me why I don't like Tuesdays, tell me why I don't like Wednesdays...' I hailed a cab and put her in, and she didn't even look at me. She told the driver her address and she went away. She never rang or text me again. I never went back to 'Meet It' but I bet Susan did.

Two days after, I met up with my ex-boyfriend and decided to give it another try. I still hated him but at least I knew what his favourite chocolate bar was and when it was his niece's birthday. I think he always knew I would be back. I went back to my old job and back to my old friends. I deleted Instagram. It's been seven months since I last saw Susan – apart from last week.

My boyfriend and I were on the top deck of the bus going to see a play in the theatre. It was nearly dark and was raining. The lights outside were blurred in the condensation on the windows and my denim jacket was damp and cold. He was on his phone talking to his friend from work about work. They were arguing and laughing, and I could smell Pot Noodles when he laughed. Then Susan got on the bus. My heart stopped dead. She saw me and put her head down but said nothing. No reaction. Nothing. She sat a few rows in front of us and I could see that same hair at the back of her neck hanging over the edge of her collar and wished I could trim it to make it neater. Nobody else on the bus or in the whole universe ever noticed or was annoyed or obsessed with that hair. Only me. I squeezed my thumb three times and wiped the window to look out.

The Kirkby Poet
Anthony McCarthy

Robert Atherton (1861-1930)

I have lived in Kirkby (Knowsley) most of my life. I had no idea until quite recently that Kirkby had its own poet. The poet concerned, Robert Atherton, was born in Victorian Kirkby.

It is a sad thought that most modern Kirkby people do not know they have a writer.

I came across a reference to Atherton by chance and decided to research his life-story and his work. The result is a project in the archives of Kirkby and Liverpool Central libraries. Here is an outline of Atherton's very interesting life.

Robert Atherton was born in Liverpool where his parents were grocers. He was orphaned very young and was handed over to farming relatives in Kirkby.

He became a ploughboy and must have thought that was to be that for the rest of his life.
He recalls that one day he had a moment of religious inspiration and decided to become a clergyman. He was laughed at, including by the Cambridge-educated, local vicar.

To enter theological college, Atherton had to teach himself Greek and Latin. No mean feat for a ploughboy with little formal schooling (this was mainly due to the fact that he missed a lot of lessons through ill-health).

He did learn those languages and went off to college. The local vicar, cynical to the last, said goodbye to him with a curt, 'I'll give it two weeks'.

But Atherton did very well at college and graduated above the average. He was in a group of middle-class types. He did feel like an outsider.

He was assigned to a parish in Cambridgeshire. There, his problems began. He upset the middle-class set in the parish by inviting farm hands to the vicarage every Sunday for a free lunch. He gave free piano lessons to the local ploughboys (and girls). He further upset the local worthies by sending his two daughters to a local school instead of the traditional prep school.

One day, he discovered 'irregularities' in the accounts of the local workhouse. He realised the worthies were a corrupt lot. He reported the corruption to the local newspaper.

Atherton was a brash Northerner: he had an instinctive dislike of middle-class hypocrisy. He detested their corruption. The paupers in the workhouse were having their food allowance cut and the money saved was unaccounted for.

The Church of England decided to get rid of him. He was charged with offences and tried in a consistory (church) court. Atherton insisted on a criminal trial, but this was rejected. He was found guilty and removed from the clergy lists.

He went back home to Kirkby. He had always been a writer and moved to Birmingham, then Manchester, to develop his work. He sold broadsheets of his work in the street.

In Manchester, he fell foul of a local politician. Once more, Atherton suspected accounting fraud. This got him into more trouble.

His wife was reported to have run off with a (horse) groom. She, and Atherton's two daughters, disappeared to America.

He was reunited with his daughters, briefly, in later life.

Atherton's work is quite lyrical. His poetry explores the issues of friendship and community solidarity. He writes about his loss of faith. He was a great Conservative but appalled by baseless snobbery.

He also wrote patriotic songs and drinking ballads.

Atherton died in 1930. He had been living in relative poverty in a barn in Kirkby.

The First Casualty of War (1982)
Anthony McCarthy

'Just check I've brought your notes. Yes, here we are. So generally, how are you?

'Fine. I've always been fine.'

'Bad start. It's all part of your recovery to acknowledge that you're ill, that's the basis of all psychotic recovery... shows insight and insight means getting better.'

'Never been unwell, you know my account of all this.'

'I know what you believe, but what a mentally-ill person believes is not the real situation.'

'I repeat again, please Mr---.'

'Corporal would be more appropriate.'

'This is a civilian hospital rank means little here besides, you were offered a military hospital and you refused.'

'For obvious reasons anyway, my rank means a lot to me. So, does my time in the Falklands.'

'Pity you can't just be happy with the victory, like all the rest.'

'I'll always support the lads I was with, most of them I'm proud to have done my bit in the fighting. But there are bigger things.'

'Post Traumatic Stress Disorder, PTSD, is a very insidious thing. It distorts your view of things; makes you believe things that didn't happen.'

'I know what happened I saw it happen, you're the one who is trying to distort.'

'If you start to get aggressive, I'll press the alarm and you'll be back on an isolation ward pumped full of sedatives. You really are your own worst enemy,
I know who the real enemy is.'

'War is such a brutal thing sends people into chaotic states of mind.'

'How would you know?'

'More of your verbal aggression I'll have to note it. It all puts back your eventual release date.'

'What do you know about war…about the noise, the screams; the bitter smell of burning bodies after a phos-phorus grenade; the red stains all over the ground and uniforms…what do you know about all that?'

'Says here, in your file, that your use of aggressive lan-guage to people trying to help you face the truth is to be held against you when any review date is set for release into the community.'

'I say again: I saw two Argentinian prisoners thrown over a cliff in cold blood. We'd had them in custody for over an hour. Some young private says, *Let's send them abseiling.* Another adds, … *Yeh….but without a rope* turns out the two Argies were half American that's the real cause of me being here.'

'We took sidewinders from the Americans…satellite intel… what would their people think if it became known we'd murdered two of their own?'

'All this has no credibility, you're a sectioned mental patient no-one will take anything you say, seriously.'

'I'll always know what happened.'

'None of this is helping your recovery you've heard stories you've put yourself into the stories these things happen.'

'Besides, you have physical symptoms of your psychosis, florid behaviour in public weak bladder control.'

'Those symptoms were induced, psychoactive drugs and diuretics in my food and drink all nicely arranged.'

'Paranoid schizophrenia, that's the official diagnosis.'

'So, medical woman how many bayonet stabs to kill a wounded Argie?.'

'More of your nonsense, so nice if you could just forget these delusions and worked towards a release date.'

'Answer is sixteen even though a wounded combatant is protected by the Geneva Convention, how about that for more murder what about human shields? Using Argie POWs as a shield as we attacked their positions and then shooting them in the back as we got to the trenches war crime enough?'

'No point in me trying to help you, I'll take my notes and…'

'By the way, hospital wards are like factory canteens full of gossip I picked up that you're the daughter of an army colonel he now advises the MOD on 'news presentation' of the Falklands Conflict how coincidental that they put you on my case.'

'I'm terminating this session you're clearly violent and aggressive. I'm recommending a transfer to a secure unit, any release date for you will be put into abeyance pending more intensive medical therapy.'

'Give my regards to the Colonel and ask him this: the Argies had British POWs why did they not harm a single one ask him to decide, who were the savages and who were the civilised ones?'

Dedicated to Tam Dalyell (1932-2017) - Tam was a Labour MP who campaigned, as a lone voice, for an investigation into war crimes by the British Military during the Falklands Campaign.

Garfield Duchamp and John Prenton
Anthony McCarthy

I thought it would be a weekend away…alone.

Just me. And a few cold beers.

And nothing else.

Instead, as I sat at the bar under a matted awning, a sun-tanned stranger approached. He was sunned but not with a holiday tan; it was the tan of someone who would much prefer to be indoors.

The stranger had a hunted look: Lord Lucan if he had been sixty years younger. At first, I tried not to notice but, clearly, he wanted to talk. To someone. At least he spoke English.

Since he sat next to me, I asked him his name.

'Which one?' he replied.

'Any name that works,' I muttered.

'Garfield Duchamp.'

'From where?'

'Depends, sometimes from the USA, sometimes not.'

One of those bar conversations you begin to regret. Still, he had something about him. Something genuine. Few of us can be harsh with genuine people. We're drawn to listen.

'Story to tell?' I asked.

'Stories,' he said. Then he bought himself a drink.

Here was his story.

He led an uneventful life in Wisconsin. Midwest. Flyover territory. A man of forty, working in an insurance office. A South American wife with a shaky grasp of English. Two kids, who he assumed were his.

It was a standard nine to five existence.

Then, one day, out for a rare walk in the country, he came across a bag. A kind of battered tool bag. He walked past it. Then, he stopped. Thought. Went back. Opened it. Life changed.

A quick count gave him a figure of quarter of a million dollars. In the highest denominations.

He thought about the cops…then he unthought about them.

He took the bag, went to the airport, took the first plane to South America and the old life was gone.

By sheer luck, he had escaped his identity. All those circumstances that tie us down into a certain place and time simply dissolved.

He had his first and last socialist thought: 'The only real freedom in this society we live in comes from having cash... dollars...more of that green paper. With this money I am able to be myself.'

In his destination city, he bought a forged passport (John Prenton) and other papers. I mean just bought them. In a bar. His money seemed to make him a lot of friends. Very quickly.

He gamed in casinos. He attracted a lot of younger ladies. Maybe, he was in better shape than he thought he was. Maybe, it had something to do with the money.

He began to feel it was a mistake to flaunt the cash, but it was too late now. He felt defined by the money. He realised the cash would free him and trap him. He had a new identity, but he still had a set of circumstances to live under.

New rules and conventions applied to him, but they were still rules and conventions.

Anyway, one of those younger ladies he attracted turned out to be the fiancée of a minor drug dealer...a nasty one.

Garfield Duchamp, alias John Prenton, was on the move again. This time 'to somewhere civilised': Lisbon.

He had a lucky escape coming through Portuguese Immigration: they found two passports on him. In two different names. He bluffed that one was a friend's. Left behind.

He found a neat place to stay: Villa Luz. Just on the edge of Alfama. Great views from the hill.

Once more to a bar. Once more, he was an overlooked stranger till he gave the impression of having some cash. After that, friends.

Some of those 'friends' were curious that he changed his name as he got drunker. They assumed he was just 'American'. Maybe, all Americans had more than one set of names.

Back in Villa Luz, he began to have a twinge of guilt. What were his wife and kids thinking, now? How would they get by?

It was three months since he had 'escaped'.

He felt increasingly uncomfortable. Had he told the person he was talking to at any moment that his name was Duchamp or Prenton? Had the lost money been reported as missing? Had his disappearance made him a suspect?

One year down the line. He was in Tangiers. He was married. How, he was not quite certain. The thing was a haze.

His new Moroccan wife spoke no English. He was literally incommunicado. He learnt that his wife was Mrs Prenton. His other wife was Mrs Duchamp.

Now he was in Istanbul. Talking to me. Asking me my name...and then asking me for other names I might be using.

I felt tired. It had been a long day in the Grand Bazar. I was leaving the next day, back to Liverpool and my normal routine.

Normal?
I began to think that word had no real meaning.

As I left the bar space, I recall he gave me a haggard look and said, 'Hope you meet yourself on the road.'

A cliché for travellers. But not for a traveller without a true identity.

Perfectly You
Mitty Ramagavigan

I don't need you to be perfect
That's impossible to be
You just be perfectly you
Cos I'll be perfectly me
But when times are tough
And you regret we ever met
Remember when I whisper
This is as good as it gets.

Insta Blues
Mitty Ramagavigan

I don't want to be you
I just don't want to be me
Your life looks more colourful
In the filtered squares I see

I try not to compare
I don't know all your stories
But from where I'm sat scrolling
I just see all the glories

I should switch off
But I'm annoyingly hooked
My battery and enthusiasm drained
My plans get overlooked.

Modern Day Motherhood
Mitty Ramagavigan

I brought you into a world
I'm not sure I like
Maddening, exhausting
So many things aren't right
With eyes full of wonder
You check things are ok
My instinct is to reassure
But too soon will come the day
When I'm not sure what I'll say...

Where Are You From?

Mitty Ramagavigan

The question I most dread
Is where are you from?
A series of responses run quickly through my head
It's more complicated than you think
What do you want to know?
A one-word answer or my life on full show.
I tick the box of Asian other
But the words hold little meaning
I was raised in London, live in Liverpool
But that's not really what you're asking.

Otherness
Mitty Ramagavigan

I was raised by others
Who believed in the state,
Who believed this country,
Could be trusted with their fate.
Who taught us to work hard,
And then harder again,
But still my otherness,
Can't be shed,

And othered I Remain.

The British Convention of Witches and Wizards

Natalie Reeves Billing

Their broomsticks were dripping with dew from the road,
Armed with a trunk and a pen and a toad.
Riding cloaks thick with green midges and fluff,
Pots fully loaded with oddments and stuff.
They come with their birch wands, rats and lizards,
To the British Convention of Witches and Wizards.

Twelve of the brightest young hags on the block,
Selected with pride from the purest witch stock.
In league with the coven, this shadowy team,
Are groomed by a warlock and witches supreme.
They summon the wind and the rain and the blizzards,
At the British Convention of Witches and Wizards.

The three potion masters — with spices and herbs,
That chant up a storm with their mystical verbs.
The seven spell weavers with silvery tongues
Who raise up the dead with their cavernous lungs.
Dark sorcerers, burning kidneys and gizzards,
At the British Convention of Witches and Wizards.

The dangerous diviners with devilish schemes,
The old elementals infecting our dreams.
They scribble on scrolls with their symbols and blots,
And put all their powers in black steaming pots.
They chop in the worms with their barbarous scissors,
At the British Convention of Witches and Wizards.

When four moons have passed, with blood drawing them home,
They put all their spells in a leather-bound tome.
So lovingly scribed onto moth-eaten pages,
A magical love that will stretch 'cross the ages.
That natural magic that's built to endure,
Will live in a true witch's heart evermore.
So, remember that place where your artistry fizzes,
The British Convention of Witches and Wizards.

John Craven
Natalie Reeves Billing

I hate John Craven!
Wouldn't you?
If John had told *you* what to do?
If Newsround was your watershed,
That had you driven off to bed.
Should John's theme be your lullaby
For heaven's sake! Would you not cry?

I hate John Craven.
Could I not?
When he came on —that was my lot!
The theme tune with that tinny bell,
That sentenced me to restless hell.
If John had you in bed at six,
Would you not crush his head with bricks?

I hate John Craven,
Always will.
While sitting on my windowsill,
I watched as all my happy mates,
Went whizzing past on roller skates.
And so, I laid upon my bed,
Forging plans to make him dead.

I hate John Craven,
I can't lie.
And he might be a decent guy,
But I can't get to sleep without

His dulcet tones to put me out.
Now every night before I dream,
My husband plays the Newsround theme.
And yes, I hear you laugh and scoff,
But John's the one that gets me off.
This loathsome man's become my haven.
Love and hate. Up yours, John Craven!

The Rise and Fall, Part One
Natalie Reeves Billing

'*It was the best of times, it was the worst of times, it was the age of wisdom, it was the age of foolishness, it was the epoch of belief, it was the epoch of incredulity, it was the season of Light, it was the season of Darkness, it was the spring of hope, it was the winter of despair, we had everything before us...*'
— A Tale of Two Cities. Charles Dickens.

Throughout my life, words and music have been my one constant companion. Everything else: a vast, shifting blob. School choirs, carol competitions, talent shows, bands, music college, poetry, diaries. Words are the well that my soul pours into. Flowing and free.

This freedom allows me to put my truth on the page. To exorcise it from my head. To purge through pen and paper. Something so inherently personal is hard to look at objectively. How can you distance yourself from your own heart? When work becomes a living breathing beast with feelings of its own, it's easy for it to get confused with your own personal validation.

But that's the life of a creative. A musician. A wordsmith. You put your baby on display and allow others to take shots at it. It's tough, but I weather it in the hope that one day, someone will look at my baby and say, 'Aww, isn't she pretty? Just like her mummy?'

I needed people to know who I was and accept it. Respect it. So, at twenty, while at music college, I started a band. We were a motley bunch. Mismatched and asymmetrical; a real bag of Revels. There was a Malteser, a toffee and–unfortunately–a raisin one, but I was the true prize. The chocolate orange. The fondant fancy. My ego was as huge as it was small. The dichotomy of superiority versus self-loathing ran parallel inside me, like a preposterous paradox. But in true Libran style, I managed to balance the two sides for quite some time. Such was my desire to break away from who I was.

The guitarist and I got together. Inevitable really. We were the songwriters. The beating heart of the band, prone to palpitating when doubt crept in. There are always going to be problems on a cellular level when anger and depression meet addiction and repression. Our union alone set the death knell ringing. But of course, I couldn't see the band for the backing singers. (And, boy, did we end up with a lot of them.)

There's a magic that comes from the combined energy of two truly broken people. We were beasts of burden laden with secrets and betrayal. But as we had different emotional mashups, mine manifested itself in deep, cavernous lows and bouts of self-harming. He had various problems, yet could always find a temporary fix in the depths of a vodka bottle.

He was the Yin to my Yang, happy to relent to the force of my will and be swept along in the fires of my ambition. I wanted out of the life I had. I tried to shift shape, and become something altogether different. Everyone else had to hold on tight or be swept aside. It was time for me to break the mould. Shed my skin and make good. Prove that I was worthy of respect and adoration.

I became our unofficial band manager. From our council house in Kensington, I'd sit at the computer for hours and hours, day after day, sending thousands of emails to thousands of companies all across the globe. 'Check out the latest single from the band, 'Bla Bla'. The ones to watch for 2004.'

I faithfully recorded the feedback into a primitive database, listing times, names and dates. Hundreds of padded envelopes flew out the door each month, 80% of them destined for London.

I had it nailed.

The system was fool proof. It was only a matter of time, and someone was going to snap us up.

The atmosphere in the band was 'familial.' We lived in each other's pockets and shared the highs and lows of the road to celebrity. It was the closest I'd ever felt to a connection in many, many years. I had brothers who looked out for me. Wouldn't hear a bad word said about me. There through thick and thin. A family that respected my ability and commitment, and I theirs.

I didn't realise it, but I'd already won. I had love. I had friends.

But then fame came knocking at the door, and I shouldn't have answered.

An email from California changed the course of our story forever. Written entirely in red ink and capitalised throughout. It shouted at us like a town crier, desperate for an audience. GREETINGS, FROM DR HENRY JONES. MARINA INVESTORS GROUP (MIG RECORDS)

A new independent label in Los Angeles wanted to sign us up. And just like that, poof, a recording contract landed in my inbox. (Along with its brother, 'Management Contract.' So, who cares if it was a massive conflict of interest?) Not me. Not when there are touring schedules attached, ticket reservations ready to go...all we had to do was sign the damned thing and pick three band representatives to jump a plane. (Well two! It went without saying that I was going!)

A week later, like wizards of old, bearing our grandparent's dust-coated cases from the 1970s, we arrived at LAX, only half believing any of this could possibly be true. Things like this don't happen in real life. Not to me anyway.

At the orientation point, it was a least an hour before anyone dared admit that Dr Henry Jones may not be coming. He may have been called to pull Indiana out of some scrape or other, who knows? But if he was here, in this bustling throng of humanity, we certainly would have seen him. A smiling, round-faced, pinstriped sporting, bow tie boasting, flat cap wearing, hulk of a man with a thick Nigerian accent would not have gone unnoticed. I half expected Jeremy

Beadle to spring out from a kiosk and escort us back to Blighty. With hotel details in hand, we hailed a cab to the Ritz Carlton and hoped it wasn't a mirage.

The Ritz Carlton in Marina Del Rey is a splendid sight indeed. Fountains, up lights, Barbie dolls and topiary. I wanted to run away, back to my rock and promptly slide under it. Drained, smelly and fearing a scam, we entered the foyer with eyes agog.

At the desk, Mrs Wide Smile was happy to tell us that there were indeed reservations, but without the relevant credit card to accompany it, she could neither confirm nor deny that they were ours. We sat on a circular sofa, watching Hollywood's finest work the space. My ragged fingernails raked tracks through the plush velvet cushions beneath me. The air, so thick with expensive perfume, made my head swirl. I prayed to a God I hadn't talked to in years. Begged him to cut me some slack. Surely this wasn't the end of our journey?

One for our enemies (I'd helped us to collect a lot of those).

My enormous ego and condescending facial expressions hadn't helped us make many muso friends. We didn't play by the unwritten rules. Go to gigs. See other bands. Hang out on the scene. Do your time. We were poncey fringe characters; our audience was made up by 5% parent and 95% hater.

So, was this what we deserved? Was I the peacock readying for a very public plucking?

Not today, it seemed. Enter Dr Jones in a cloud of Armani. An army of followers fussing behind him, doffing and bowing; tripping over themselves to be useful. *Coming to America,* came to my mind. His robes were exquisite. He looked and smelt the part. A truly impressive specimen. There'd be no need for apology or excuse; he didn't waste time with such things. We would later learn that this was the start of his manipulation. His technique. Dr Jones started small. 'Make them wait. Keep them hungry.'

Well, we were starving. He could've asked me to jump on one arm and bark like a dog. Success was in sight, and I wasn't about to let it go.

For The Rise and Fall Part Two and more on our American dream, featuring Mike Tyson, Michael Jackson and Stevie Wonder, visit: www.echoesofabuse.com

The Boy with the Black Hair
Natalie Reeves Billing

The boy with the black hair knew nothing of love.
He lived in a harsh, unforgiving cavern carved into
the mountainside at the edge of the Stone Woods. No
birds graced the air above with their song. No animals
dared search the petrified forests for scraps. No people
came near.
For why should they?
The earth was dead. The heart of the land had ceased
its beating many years ago. No one knew why. No
one cared.
Only black flowers ever grew there.
And the rot was creeping. Inching its way up the
foothills. Threatening the wooden village above.

The boy with the black hair knew nothing of laughter.
He couldn't remember how he'd come to be in this place.
He had no name but no one to speak it if he had one.
A small pile of bones at the entrance to his dismal lair,
the only evidence of his lonely midnight meals.
He dined alone, unloved and unheard of, in that
wild place.

The boy with the black hair knew nothing of speech.
He had no need for language. He conversed with no
one. He learnt nothing but the hard lessons of trial and
error, played out against the barren wilderness.
His cries brought help from nowhere. His tears brought
comfort from no one.

His only companion, a grimy doll. Soft in body, legs and
arm. A face— cold and stern—yet hauntingly beautiful.

But sometimes he—for no reason at all—felt compelled
to pull it tight to his chest and hold that strange effigy
tight in his arms.
Something stirred then inside him. A thing that fluttered
deep in his chest, rare and unfamiliar. Sharply painful,
yet light and beautiful.

The boy with the black hair knew nothing of life.
And life knew nothing of him.

Wee Little Stool
Nina T

'She'll be grand, GRAND. I know you're worried the girls won't see her when they are playing and might knock her over but, see now, I've got this wee little stool - very discreet mind - that she can sit on in the corner of the playground tucked away from everyone…no one will even notice…she'll be fine.'

This 'wee little stool' was an old wooden church stool that the head, Sister Mary Agnes, had the school caretaker saw the legs off so that it was low enough for me to sit on. He had pimped it up with several slaps of bright blue paint and then 'discreetly' stencilled my name on the seat…in BIG CAPS…in YELLOW…TWICE! You know, just in case someone else dared claim it as their own or so it could be returned to its rightful owner should, God forbid, any wrong'un try and steal it.

The stool weighed more than I did and there were cracks all over the seat where the aged wood had split, which bit me on the bum each time I sat on it. Hardly steal-worthy swag but I didn't care cos it was going to keep me safe and it was mine, all mine; it said so in big letters.

I sat on my stool as my friends circled around me, blocking out the chaos of the playground.

'Right, c'mon then, who's first?'

I stood up as the highly complex decision-making technique began. 'Dip, dip, dip, my blue ship…' I took my starting position, arms stretched out to the sides, shoulder height like the sign of the cross. '…O. U. T. spells OUT!'

I felt a friendly arm either side of me scoop under each armpit before lifting me high into the air. I blinked quickly taking everything in; it was so much brighter and louder up here…dark to light.

My scarred, chubby legs dangled in mid-air - Don't Care, Don't Care - it was so strange seeing the world from this height. As I drew a deep breath which tasted of hairspray and strawberry Hubba Bubba chewing gum, I turned to my friend on my left whose nervous smile hid behind gleaming braces which grinned back at me unconvincingly. I could tell she was as terrified/excited as I was for what lay ahead.

I smiled at my friend on my right hoping for some reassurance that everything was going to be ok. Nothing. She had her game face on, staring straight ahead, fully focused on the tatty old water pipes 50 yards in front which marked the half way point…this was no play time, this shit was serious…Great Britain was depending on us to bring back an Olympic gold medal. The only movement was her jaw as she chewed her gum in time to the countdown…

'Three (clack)…Two (clack)…One(clack)…GO!'

And we were off, running, together, RUNNING, arm in arm, my friends carrying me full speed through the playground so I could feel what it was like to keep up with them. As the enthusiastic cheers from our friends faded into the distance, sounds of panting and giggling filled my ears. The girls, giving it their all, sprinted completely out of time with each other in new shoes (which they were going to grow into) and failed to cling onto their feet as they flapped dangerously up and down to the halfway mark.

I'd like to think I was the cox in this odd li'l set up. I thought of myself as a sandwiched bundle of hope and optimism, motivating my team with worldly wise words of advice and guidance to steer them in the right direction, but I blame the g-force for putting paid to that. In truth, we were just a holy mess, no plan, no clue what we were doing. We were all over the place but giving it everything we had so as not to let each other down.

Each out of sync step pounding on the ground caused me to jiggle in between them uncontrollably, but I never feared that I would fall. I kept everything I owned tightly clenched as I was convinced my insides were going to be shaken out with every mistimed beat. I visualised a trail of my vital organs strewn across the playground marking out our journey, but at least we could follow that trail, which would lead us back to our friends Hansel and Gretel style.

'Kick it!' they gasped. 'KICK IT!'

I braced myself to play my vital part, which was to kick the water pipes as a sign we were halfway home. It was the furthest point away from the head's office we could find as Christ-knows-what Sister would have thought if she had looked out and seen the vacant wee little stool and then a shortarse flying full speed passed her window, not dissimilar to *The Snowman's* famous 'Walking In The Air' scene, if The Snowman had been smacked off his face on speed chasing his next fix.

KICK! The red flaky paint from the old water pipes stuck to my shoe as we spun 180 degrees. We were heading back towards the finish line of mismatched misfits jumping up and down like lunatics.

I could tell I was getting heavier as the lip biting increased and the speed decreased, but the girls weren't giving up. They had a steady rhythm going now, swinging their free arms wildly in perfect time with each other to keep momentum but mainly to knockout any girl-shaped obstacle that dared get in our way. We were going for a PB here.

Once my eyeballs had stopped bouncing around in their sockets, I could finally focus on the rest of the playground from my unusual vantage point.

Now you see me, I thought. Now you see me.

I don't think anyone batted an eyelid to be honest; they were far too busy making up dance routines whilst singing the lyrics from the latest Smash Hits magazine. Others were too busy trying to unknot the string of their Coca Cola yo-yos after several failed attempts to 'walk the dog' to even care, but I was there.

The rest of the playground noise was drowned out by the excited whooping and cheering from our friends which carried us on towards the finish line. We were nearly there but the girls were flagging and moving in slow motion. I imagined this is exactly how we would look on the big screen when they replayed this magnificent feat on the Olympic highlights.

The rhythmic thumping in my ears beat in time to Starship's 'Nothing's Gonna Stop Us Now' which they would undoubtedly play over the supercut of our best bits. It was reassuring to hear my heart, at least my body had managed to hold on to one vital organ. My minds montage was soon ruined by the backing singers either side of me freestyling with wonderful lyrics like…

'Wait, I can't breathe.'
'Me arm's gone dead.'
'Am gonna drop her.'
'Ave lost me fuckin' shoe.'
…as we stumbled into the finish line cushioned by a bunch of smiling idiots.

I was lowered safely back onto my wee little stool…light to dark…before the girls collapsed either side of me into the gravel, crumpled, sweaty bodies gasping for air in between laughing and fixing their scrunchies.

We had made it!

I looked round at the red beaming faces which were, once again, level with mine - eye to eye - although my eyes

disappeared as a big, stupid smile took up all the room on my chubby face.
'What was our time?'

'Er, dunno…she said she was cou-'

'No…you said you were…I thought you were countin-'

'Aaarrrggghhh!'

'Right, our turn now…keep count this time, Dickhead!'

And once again, I am lifted into the air…dark to light… before my aching arms have time to recover, by another pair of fresh-faced friends. Limbered up and raring to go, they are determined to outdo the others but know it's only about making it back to the wee little stool.

Pieces in Pieces
Nina T

Begin at the corners, work outside in
Picture near perfect, separation so thin
Watch as the pieces just fall into place
Connecting together leaving one tiny space.

Bite off the edges, hit hard with a fist
Crumble to pieces, don't try to resist
Twisting and turning, is it all just pretence
Trying to be what you're not, the only defence.

Reach for the edges, hold tight with no grip
Slight shake of the picture, the pieces will slip
Forced into spaces you're desperate to fill
But the gap's just too wide, resentment will spill.

So far yet so near, it's all such a shame
Picture near perfect but no one's to blame
Be brave just move on, accept this defeat
Go search for the picture your piece will complete.

Show, Don't Tell
Nina T

I have always been disappointed by the lack of real disabled performers and entertainers appearing in mainstream popular culture, particularly television, as this is supposed to be the closest reflection of the diverse society we live in. But is it a true representation?

I was excited to hear recently on the BBC, *Ouch!* (a disability podcast) an interview with Tim Renkow, a stand-up comedian with cerebral palsy, promoting his new BBC Three show, *Jerk*, which he created, co-wrote and stars in. As well as the boxset available on BBC iPlayer, *Jerk* was also shown Monday nights on BBC One at 11.05pm after the popular *Fleabag* in the new BBC Three timeslot.

There are many similarities between the dark comedies, *Fleabag* and *Jerk*, shown back to back on BBC One in March. Both are written by and starring their creators. Both shows are supported by a strong cast (*Lost Voice Guy* – Lee Ridley - who over one million people voted for as the winner of *Britain's Got Talent 2018* makes a genius cameo in *Jerk*). Both are pushing boundaries as far as they can possibly get away with. Both disarm with humour then sucker punch with reality through funny but honest takes on the tragedies of real life.

Television executives are constantly crying out for new and interesting stories told from a unique perspective. Well, here they are - right here - *Jerk* is full of them. The joys of job seeking as a disabled person. The minefield of online dating as a disabled person. Playing un-PC pranks on the non-disabled. Hilarious stories boldly told with a wicked twist through the eyes of someone who knows exactly what it's like to be perceived as 'different' in the real world.

But where is the advertising to promote this new innovative show? Why is it not receiving the same level of support as other BBC Three programmes or included in the iPlayer regularly shown on the BBC? Surely the BBC should be proud of commissioning such a ground-breaking show, so why not equally invest in the all-important advertising that's essential for new programmes to be seen? How can a show gain a bigger audience if you don't show the audience it is there?

Apart from the BBC *Ouch*! interview (featured on a disability platform), I haven't seen or heard any other advertising for *Jerk* - not on television, radio, billboards or buses - unlike its BBC Three counterparts *Fleabag, Cuckoo, Man like Mobeen* and *This Country*, which are regularly promoted across the media. I watched with interest, the BBC One viewing figures for both Monday night shows - *Fleabag* averaged about 1.5 million over the course of the series and *Jerk* approximately 600,000. Both BBC Three comedies, one shown right after the other, similar in many ways, yet a significant drop in audience ratings.

Viewing figures reflect how well a show has been received and undoubtedly impact on its re-commissioning potential. But is it fair to measure audience figures for *Jerk* against its counterparts when there is such disparity between the level of promotion the shows were afforded? How can meaningful decisions be made on future programming if it's difficult to determine the real reason behind the ratings? Did the mainstream audience simply not want to see a show like *Jerk* on television or did they even know it was there? As yet, there are no plans to re-commission *Jerk*.

Disabled people on mainstream television tend to be featured in factual/reality programmes. Where are the dramas and the comedies displaying the talents of disabled people? Where are the shows led by disabled entertainers showcasing the unique and valuable contribution they can make to television given the opportunity? Where are the role models encouraging other disabled artists/performers to be part of the mainstream?

In the March issue of *Broadcast*, it was interesting to read an article by Joanna Tilley entitled 'CDN chair calls for 'step change' in diversity monitoring.' It highlighted the 'Doubling Disability' pledge major broadcasters BBC, ITV, Channel 4, Channel 5 and Sky have signed up to in a bid to increase diversity in front of and behind the camera. Whenever I hear of these new initiatives to encourage inclusivity in the mainstream, I am hopeful that they do make a long-term difference and the successful outcome will be seen on television. This would give a more realistic picture of society today as, more than ever, the audience is wanting to see honest and truthful representations of themselves on the big screen.

But this incentive won't have an impact if it's just about enhancing diversity statistics within the media and motivating broadcasters to be 'seen' to be positive about equality by hitting targets like 'Doubling Disability' through box ticking, quota meeting, and data gathering exercises. I wonder if the audience will see the results of this initiative reflected on our TV screens or just hear of the results via numbers and statistics from monitoring systems?

Top quality television like *Jerk* warrants equal promotion and to be seen by a larger audience. I hope that broadcasters show their commitment to improving diversity in mainstream television by treating programmes equally from commissioning through to vital advertising. Disabled performers deserve the opportunity to show their talent and the significant impact they can have on the entertainment industry.

In the Bag
Nina T

Out and about on the mainstream social scene, I often think of myself as a celebrity. I too get stared at, slyly photographed without permission and subjected to inappropriate and personal questions from complete (mostly intoxicated) strangers.

Over the years I've developed a genius cognitive coping strategy. I pretend the unwanted attention is because the idiots think I'm famous and are mistaking me for the likes of Abbey Clancy (Ok, Ok, Janette Krankie), Jennifer Ellison (especially when I hit that dance floor) or one of Wayne Rooney's many (but surprisingly young) conquests.
It seems the only difference between me and fellow high-profile celebs (besides money, fame, tax dodging) is what's in our bags.

Books, copious beauty products, numerous lip balms, phones, diaries and crystals tumble from the bags of the famous as *British Vogue* asks celebrities like Jane Fonda, Victoria Beckham and Helen Mirren to reveal the essentials they carry around on a daily basis for their feature 'In the Bag.'

Whilst I wait for *British Vogue* to come a-knocking at my door asking me to spill the contents of 'My Life In A Bag' onto the floor - I have a mooch through the essentials I carry around. As a physically disabled social butterfly navigating through this big, bad world prepared for 'every' eventuality – it's a survival kit that Bear Grylls would be proud of.

- Extendable stick - to reach things (or 'accidentally' trip/ poke rude people aka dickheads).

- Adjustable luggage strap - to lasso round out of reach door handles and heave (or for snaring unsuspecting hotties at the local hoedown).

- Industrial strength suction cups - to attach to glass doors with out of reach handles and heave (or attach to hands/feet for scaling up the outside of glass buildings like a Scouse Spider-Woman when the accessible lift inside is 'Out of Order'…again).

- Foldable stool - to use as a stepping stone to bigger and better things.

- Spare Tena pants - in case I go through the two pairs I'm already wearing (on the outside of my clothes btw, Wonder Woman style) waiting for the non-disabled person/people inside the disabled toilet to finish changing their clothes/having sex. To be honest, disabled loos are bigger than most changing rooms/hotel rooms in the nearby Travelodge so, fair play.

- Shewee (optional) - as above re: usual disabled toilet situation but note this can be confiscated by jobsworth security as often considered a lethal weapon hence the need for aforementioned backup Tena pants.

So, if you need to survive out in the wild then I'm your girl - just don't come to me for lip gloss, money or a tampon as my *Mary Poppins* meets *Fifty Shades of Grey* clutch bag has only got room for the most essential of essentials.

What's in your bag?

Just a Thought
Nina T

Haters are lovers who just don't understand
Show them your truth, give them your hand
Show them that difference is nothing to fear
We all have the right to find happiness here.

The Stranger
Karen Bryony Rose

'Help me,' the man says. The words halt my stride. An unfamiliar plea wrapped in an unmistakable voice. My stomach drops. It can't be him.

'Help me!' he yells. I turn sharply and barely notice the chill wind at my back for the figure lain across the bench in front of me. He's smaller than I remember, but his deep-set eyes behind thick brown framed glasses hold the same contempt. With an unshaven slack chin and a forehead scored with lines, the years have left their mark. A long, creased khaki coat pools around his form and over loose faded jeans. The laces on his scuffed boots are undone.

The noise of the city seems to fade, replaced by the sound of my increasing heartbeat. No longer am I a thirty-year-old woman on her way to meet her husband; instead I'm eight years old, fighting the urge to run. Anxiety settles in a tight band across my chest and I pull my coat about me and cross my arms. I want to disappear. The same suffocating feeling of dread on hearing his heavy tread on the stairs threatens to overcome me now. It's like I'm wearing the cowed demeanour of the child I used to be.

'Help me, please.' He pauses. 'Jenny.' My name added, as an afterthought. So now he needs somebody. He used to whisper between swigs of lager, 'People are only out for what they can get, they only want to know your business, we don't need nobody.' He cheated me out of what he lost when he was a boy – a proper father.

I shift my weight to my other foot and glance around the quiet street, with its tall glass-fronted buildings. Later people will spill onto the pavement from these bars and restaurants.

He makes to move, and I freeze, barely daring to blink. Clutching his stomach, he winces with each movement in an effort to sit upright. The last time I'd seen him he'd been confident and in control. Now he's on a deserted street with no one around but me. Peering up at me, like a frightened child, I catch a glimpse of the boy he once was, snared by anguish and grief over the death of his dad. His mum had held her grief close, like a treasured possession. And so, he'd grown to be a child in a man's body, never learning what it was to love despite loss.

I turn away, not sure I can deal with this right now. 'What, you're just gonna walk on?' he spits, finally reaching a seated position. He leans back on the bench, breathing heavily. He's going nowhere fast, I think. My breathing quickens and heat rises to my chest constricting my throat. 'I should,' I force through dry lips.

His eyes meet mine. 'You'd just walk on and leave me here?' he says, coughing loudly. No one would blame me for walking away right now. He made sure fear occupied the space where love should have been. I've earned the right to walk away. 'Don't put the blame on me,' I say, finally, my fists balled and heat building behind my eyes. I blink quickly to stop the tears. 'It's always someone else's fault, isn't it?' I blurt out. Usually mine or Mum's. His way of

absolving himself of responsibility for his actions. *Bastard.*
He shakes his head and sneers. 'Oh yeah, I've heard it all
before. You sound like your bloody mother.'

He gets to his feet unsteadily, pulling himself to full height.
A piece of folded white paper drifts to the ground and
instinctively I bend to pick it up. The logo of the local
hospital and the words 'prognosis' and 'terminal' seem to
float before my eyes. A bud of something like pity blooms
in my chest and heat spreads across my face. No, this guilt
is not mine. I mustn't betray what Mum went through by
feeling sorry for him.

'Give that to me,' he says, snatching the paper from my
hand and releasing stale breath laced with alcohol.

'Go on then, leave me alone,' he sneers. 'Go back to your
mum like you always did. I don't need you.' A frown dis-
solves on his forehead and a cold mask shrouds his face. I
know then – in that moment - that this is over. Even now,
with death ahead of him, he hasn't changed. A wave of
sadness rises to my throat and hot tears cloud my vision.
The life he wasted and the family he took for granted a
mere shimmer on the tears. There's nothing left for either
of us. I turn my back and walk away.

The Fall
Karen Bryony Rose

In the fall from
wakefulness to slumber
lies the veracity of my soul.

The day disrobes,
unfurling to the ground exposing
a spirit unburdened.

What matters reveals itself,
fears press their case
wanting to be heard.

Released from distraction
life's pressures are held aloft
in temporary reprieve.

My mind soars on borrowed wings,
and sight holds a clarity
unattainable in wakefulness.

Green Eyed Monster
Karen Bryony Rose

Cara fastened her red shoes, feeling the buckle slip from her clammy fingers. The venue might be unfamiliar, the town unknown, but the ritual was always the same: shoes on last, left foot first. Somehow the habit helped her to shift headspace. 'Ten minutes to showtime, Cara,' John whispered behind her, his hand lingering on her arm and his warm breath on her neck sending her thoughts into disarray. She smiled. She'd find him after the show, when an adrenalin-fuelled urgency would overpower her, and they'd share a private encore. She couldn't remember how their affair had begun but it had been inevitable. She'd invested her trust in him for the success of her career and his star had ascended with her every triumph.

The fluttering in her chest seemed to move in unison with the bubble of voices beyond the heavy deep sapphire curtain. The lights above the cavernous stage beamed a cascade of rainbow waves across a sea of faces. Cara's feet had danced the Liverpool Empire's stage a thousand times in her dreams. And now she was ending her solo nationwide tour here, in her home city.

Her career had begun a few miles away. She remembered the draughty church hall had smelled of dust but her first pair of patent red dancing shoes with their stubby heels had been perfect. During those first dance lessons, Cara had marvelled at the effect of movement and music on her awkward limbs. And how her body had responded to the moves as though it'd merely needed a reminder. She was born to dance.

Cara gave a sigh at the memory and peered around the heavy curtain again. Through the triangle of darkness her mum's face appeared, lit briefly by the coloured lights. They hadn't spoken in years. Cara moved to get a better view. Her mum, Ruth, was in the front row, dressed to the nines and with a face that could turn lava to ice. Her mum had withdrawn her affections for Cara with every passing year.

She remembered the night when she had lost her for ever. Dance class was almost at an end when her mum had made an unexpected entrance at the back of the hall. Her dad usually collected her from class. Cara was at the centre of the front row of smiling girls who moved in unison to a lively beat. Sweat glistened on the contours of her chest and there were strands of hair stuck to her forehead. With her dad's dark hair and olive skin and her mum's high cheekbones, Cara stood out among the other girls.

'That's all now, girls. See you next week!' the dance teacher Joanna said, beaming with pride, her round of applause echoing around the hall.

The girls scattered towards their waiting mums; their faces upturned like flowers basking in maternal praise. Cara dashed forwards, trying to read her mum's face which was set like stone. 'Oh,' she uttered through tight lips. 'You light up a room now.'

Cara shrank from her mum's accusatory tone, as the words echoed around the empty room. She made to talk but shrivelled beneath her mum's narrowed glare as hot shame burned beneath her skin. She had felt rudderless, as though she'd been cast adrift on an unforgiving sea.

Her mum had been cold after that night. She'd filled her diary with gym classes, spa visits or other self-maintenance tasks. Cara had assumed her mum enjoyed her pampering sessions but as the weeks passed by she'd noticed a dullness expanding in her mum's eyes each time she returned.

A month was all it took for her mum to convince her dad to pull strings and send their daughter to dance school in London.

After a few years, her dad had grown immune to her mum's insecurity and her mum had sought the attention of someone new. They'd split up after that. Cara realised she'd been sent away so that her mum wouldn't have to share her dad's adoring gaze. In her teenage years she'd seen the same guarded looks on the faces of her friends whenever Cara spoke to their boyfriends. As her career began to soar, friends stopped inviting her out, unable to cope with her fame and the men's lingering looks in Cara's direction.

With each rejection Cara worked harder and went on to win competition after competition. If she couldn't be loved for herself, she would be loved for her dancing. She stepped beyond the curtain and took her place beneath the spotlight, the only place she'd truly belonged.

106 Liscard – Wallasey
Karen Bryony Rose

Greasy hair fastened back in haste,
Apathy on her careworn young face.
With her hooded gaze and vacant stare,
Her eyes have seen too much to care.
Slack-jawed and catching flies,
Her painted mouth full of his lies.
She jiggles the pram with one hand,
To quell her baby's demand.
On her phone she replies to his text:
'Got your cans - *Stella* and *Becks*.'
No reply as she chews her nails,
She taps her foot and the baby wails.
Beyond the window buildings fly past.
Takeaways, bookies - they won't last.
Same tired town, different name
What did it matter? They're all the same.

Log Out to Tune In
Karen Bryony Rose

I fell into the technology trap again recently. Reader, I regressed. Lured by the sweeping tide of the Brexit saga, my phone demanded my attention with every BBC News update and every WhatsApp group message. Every high-pitched notification sent my stomach into a spiral. What's happened now? I'd wonder, as my fingers flew over the screen and a cold creeping dread settled in my gut.

Slowly the little pockets of quiet in my day disappeared. The magic of waking up early and lingering over breakfast, letting my mind wander on the commute to work, people watching in a beer garden as the evening sun sank below the trees leaving pink streaks and marshmallow clouds in its wake. Once again technology had me in its grip and I'd tuned out of real life.

Over a year ago, I was grappling with the pretty baffling symptoms of an undiagnosed health condition. Brain-fogged days dissolved into fitful nights where worries lurked in the shadows of my dreams. My mind and body were gripped by fatigue.

My friend Jen came to the rescue, suggesting a day out to the seaside. It was to be a vintage day out to Llandudno, and she'd planned the works: ice creams on the pier, a trip to the amusement arcades and fish and chips on the Prom. The old Pier bustled with holidaymakers with pink shoulders and tan lines, women in short shorts and men wearing socks with sandals. A man dressed in a pirate outfit with a bird of prey perched on his shoulder strutted past the stalls selling donuts and buckets and spades.

As I leaned against the wrought iron railings with an ice cream in one hand, and my phone in the other, I realised I hadn't taken one photograph or looked out to sea since we'd arrived. Instead my mind had been a merry-go-round of recurring worries and Twitter feeds, Gmail and WhatsApp groups. I wasn't taking a break at all. Trying to maintain my online life as well as my real life was evidently unrealistic at this time.

I gave my phone to Jen for the rest of the day and forced myself to tune into my surroundings, to jump off the merry-go-round. I let myself breathe in the scents of summer: sun cream and candyfloss. I watched the burning orb in the cloudless sky cast dappled light through the trees. I strolled along the Prom that shimmered in the hazy midday sun and ate fish and chips and dodged the dive-bombing seagulls.

On the journey home I downsized my online life. And I know that I can do it again.

Here are some quick tips for when you need to take a technology break.

Review your social media – mute, unfollow, disengage
Take a look at your social media accounts. Are most of your interactions positive or negative or a mix of both? Ask yourself if another argument with someone you don't

know is the best use of your time? If your timeline is a barrage of negativity that makes your hackles rise every time you log in, then it's time to weed through your followers.

Your time is precious – say yes to people
Who hasn't logged into Twitter with the intention of checking their feed and replying to a few DMs, only to realise that two hours have passed? Most of those trips down the Twitter rabbit hole are a waste of your time. Remember, when we say yes to one thing, we are saying no to another. Say yes to catching up with friends, going for a walk, or discovering a new restaurant instead.

Go for a walk – your mental health will thank you for it
Last year I took on Country Walking Magazine's 'Walk 1,000 miles in 2018' challenge and let me tell you, fresh air and a change of scene had a magical effect on my mood. It doesn't matter how far or how fast you walk, what's important is that you move forwards.

Set phone boundaries especially before bed
I used to be useless at this but these days, come bedtime, you won't find my phone next to my bed. Only a few possessions occupy that sacred space: my current read and a notebook and pen.

Small changes like these can help you regain space to notice the little things that make you happy. To tune in to your present. For a while you'll have major FOMO, but this will dissipate. You'll be spending more time with family and friends, having better quality sleep, powering through your to-do list, taking the dog for another walk, finding ten minutes' peace for a relaxing bath *or* maybe allowing yourself to do nothing at all!

Where Are We Now?
The Mouse Killer
Vicky M Andrews

It's 4:30am and I'm standing in the garden in the rain, wearing a fluffy dressing gown, unlaced boots and a rubber glove. One hand is holding the gown closed to protect my modesty, the other a dead mouse by its tail. The night air is warm and earthy from moss and rotting deadwood under the grandest old trees, their leaves whispering to each other from giant limbs in dark corners. I tread across the boggy lawn and fling the mouse into a bush. It lands star-shaped on a branch at the top, inches from my eyeline.

'For fuck's sake,' I mutter, scanning the windows behind me to see if anybody in the house is watching this circus. A car horn honks rudely from the next street, the engine chugging loudly over drunk laughter and goodbyes. I wait for the safety of silence and lean into the shrubbery to retrieve the mouse and make a second attempt to toss it out of sight. I hold the thin, rubbery tale in between my gloved thumb and forefinger, its weightless little body hanging upside down, arms outstretched like a cheerleader, before spinning off into the undergrowth for a second time. I'm not exactly sure where it landed. I peer in. No sign. Operation Mouse complete.

I creep back into the hallway, slowly bolting the back door. I leave the rubber glove in the bathroom sink and head back into the bedroom. The *Milk Tray* man has nothing on me. 'Sorted?' my girlfriend mumbles into her pillow with half-open eyes. Before I can reply, she lets out a little snore. I take off my rodent disposal outfit and slide back into the comforting warmth of soft bed covers. The cat, we'll call him 'Mr P' to protect his identity, sits up and blinks, releasing an enormous yawn. 'What's up?'

I never thought he'd be a killer. Our previous cat, Oriel, was a laid-back old lady, content to spend her last days watching the world from the window. She was old: nineteen in cat years which is equivalent to ninety-two human years. On the day she left us, we banged her breakfast bowl at 7am as usual but she didn't come. I hadn't heard her make a sound in the night and I'd like to think she went peacefully, but I don't know if death is ever kind.

Family pets had always been dealt with by my parents, so I called them for advice. 'I don't...know...what...to...do with her,' I wailed. 'How hard is the ground outside?' my dad had asked. It was January, snowing and bloody freezing. I didn't own a spade and I had serious doubts that the neighbours would support a pet cemetery in the communal garden.

The vets said they'd hold her in a freezer, and she'd go in a van down to a crematorium in the Midlands; the ashes would come back in a week or so. She hadn't travelled that far in life and it didn't seem appropriate. A slightly hysterical phone call and a few hundred quid later and her ashes came home from an equine crematorium that same day.

I hurt more from that loss than any human death. I drowned my heartache in gin and wept over stories of abandoned animals on Facebook. I tried to look at the positives and told myself that life would be better without a dependent. No expensive vets' bills, early wake-up calls or surprise fur balls in your slippers. The freedom to go on holiday when you like and to travel the world, guilt-free. Hell, I could even get a dog if I wanted to.

It was three months before Mr P came home with us from the animal shelter. I never thought he'd be a hunter. He'd been abandoned on the streets, injured by a car and recovered from a fractured leg, torn face and pellet wounds to his chest. He was cute, handsome and needy: perfect.

The first time he brought a rat home I didn't believe he'd killed it himself.

'It looks pretty stiff, must have been already dead when he found it,' I reassured my girlfriend. It was an adult rat with soaking wet fur, ragged claws and tombstone teeth. Just looking at it made my skin crawl. Its tail felt like gnarly rope; I picked it up with some gardening gloves, dangled it into a plastic bag and away into the outside bin.

The next week brought more rain, another present dropped at the window and one on the garden path. Was it a plague on my house, a warning from the Mafia or a case of the vermin suicides? 'Sounds like you need to call RentoKill,' said my mum, unhelpfully.

With a holiday on the horizon we took Mr P to the local cattery. 'Don't worry about his back leg, it just looks a bit odd because he had a car accident,' my girlfriend explained to the owner. 'Just to clarify...he wasn't actually driving the car,' I pointed out with a chuckle. 'He can't drive. Because he's a cat.' I always managed to labour the point beyond funny.

Two weeks in the slammer and a break from my bad jokes seemed to pacify his hunting instinct for a bit, but it was the calm before the storm. The sound of yowling came calling from the garden again and this time a little mouse had come for tea. 'You're not bringing that in,' I said, pulling the curtains closed as he held it in his mouth like a gimp ball.

The next morning, a military scale clean-up was launched to clear the crime scene before the kids upstairs saw it.

'It's good to know I can count on you if I ever need to dispose of a human body,' I said to my girlfriend, as she put the gloves and bleach back in the cupboard and flicked the kettle on.

'In Australia, they protect their wildlife by keeping domestic cats in outside cages,' she said, crunching on a biscuit. 'Just a thought.'

But the twist in this tale is yet to come. Before his last moments on earth, our bush mouse had arrived as a passenger at my window, confused and scared but still very much alive. His little heart had ticked like a wind-up toy as the curtains opened for his big moment. The cat looked at the mouse, the mouse looked at me, and I looked back at them both, eyeing up who might make the first move. I was determined to save this innocent creature, so I opened the window, pulled the cat inside and chucked him on the bed.

'What the hell's going on?' my girlfriend mumbled.

'He's got a mouse,' I said. 'But it's alive!' As I turned around to close the window, the mouse made a frantic dash to get inside. I reached up and pushed the wooden frame down to block the cat's exit but instead it slammed onto the mouse's back, trapping him. After a few seconds, he stopped struggling and closed his eyes and I knew I had killed him.

'I'm sorry, Mr Mouse. It was an accident,' I whisper to myself now, lying back in bed, with Operation Mouse complete.

I close my eyes and try to block out the awful feelings of guilt, while the cat makes himself comfortable on my feet on top of the blankets.

'Mouse killer,' he laughs and curls his tail around his body to go to sleep.

Waking Up
Martin Russo

A cry from outside broke my night's sleep. It sounded like
a child? A young girl perhaps? I looked out of my bedroom
window and saw nothing but darkness. Another cry and it
shook around the park and vibrated against my ear with
a sharp whip-like crack. It was raw, tense and screeched
against the quiet. It sounded human but maybe it was
something else?

I sat up, shook off the blanket and then stood. Its warmth
drifted off out the window and soon the cold started to
bite. My breath was struggling to keep up.

What was that? I opened the window wider but all I could
see was a black sheet of darkness staring back at me. The
only reminder of the outside world was a whiff of fresh
green shoots, scented tulips and jasmine hanging in the
thick damp air.

I went back to bed, pulled the duvet over and lay on my
left side. I waited. I could not face taking a step outside, not
knowing what was out there. It could be risky. I might be
injured. I might not be able to help, and I might get hurt.
I took in a deep breath. I closed my eyes.

I turned to my right side. I lay awake for two hours but
heard no more cries. I switched to the left side and still I
could not relax and rest. My body was tuned in to hear
another cry, and no amount of turning could help me sleep.

The minute I dozed off it struck again.

It was followed by a succession of high-pitched shrieks from around the west side of the park. Each one grew louder than the last and they sounded like distress calls.

I sat up again. It could have just been teenagers in the park. But I had an element of doubt, an itch that something was not quite right. Something or someone was in danger.

I got up, put my tracksuit and trainers on and left the house. I followed the path in the garden and climbed over the wooden fence and entered the park.

My feet landed on the soft grass. The darkness pushed against the overhanging trees and my vision was limited. The moon drew a line of light along the footpath. I walked up the familiar lane as I had a thousand times before but could not hear anything.

A rustle of leaves up ahead and a grey squirrel ran across my path. I stopped and watched it climb up the tree.

My hands started to sweat, and the air was damp, cold with a pungent smell of mulch.

I turned left and stepped under a long branch and moved closer to a small cluster of bushes. I couldn't see anything clearly.

'Hello?' I called out.

No response. I heard a crack of a branch ahead. The trees blocked out the moonlight. I continued to walk past the first set of trees, through some bushes and then my foot got caught on one of the bramble bushes. I tugged and pulled, but it was stuck. My top got tangled up in another branch.

I was locked in with the brambles. I heard a loud cry. I started to unzip my tracksuit jacket. There was that same shriek again, moving closer and closer and getting louder. I was shaking hard to get my top off, but I lost my footing and fell headfirst into the bramble bushes.

One of the branches scratched my arm and pierced my skin. A sharp pain flashed up my arm. 'Ouch!' I cried. Another bramble scraped across my forehead. It felt like a kitchen knife had been run over my head. Numb at first, but then a sudden punch of pain lit up across my forehead and it stung and started throbbing. A small warm drop of blood dripped from my arm but luckily not my forehead.

Another screech, only closer. Loud like a short confident bark. Less human more animal. I could smell warm raw breath. I was trapped. The dark cold air left only a shadow of movement. A second later, I heard a growl, a puff of breath against my skin and they were pushing up against me. I stayed still and quiet.

A sudden gust of wind opened up a gap in the trees and the moon put a spotlight on me. I looked below my leg to see sharp pointed white teeth. The jaws crunched on the bramble bushes and then I could move my leg. I was free.

It looked like a fox, but it was dark. A smaller cluster of them stood behind her. The silver moonlight flashed on her face; her eyes were locked on me. I breathed in and sat up. A second later, one of them popped out from her side and let out a shriek. I smiled.

I got up and ran back over the fence, cleaned up and got back into bed.

I drifted off to sleep as the sun slowly moved up in the blue sky and the birdsong filled the air with light.

Dione Island
Martin Russo

Trekking over a rock face, back towards the forest, Sarah
slips and falls down a crevice. Her rucksack stocked full
of their food supplies, battery chargers and maps, catches
the sides and leaves her dangling face down into a dark
hole below.

'You have got to climb on top of the bag!' screamed Jane.

Sally tries to pull off a nearby branch to help reach her,
but it is too tough to break. Sarah flips herself up and on
top of the bag, lodging her feet against the wall. Jane is
stretched out to grab her, while Sally secures her footing
and holds Jane's ankles tightly.

A quick jump but Sarah clips Jane's fingers. Another jump
and no contact. The bag slides further down. She takes a
deep breath and jumps again and locks onto Jane's hand.
They pull her up.

Sarah falls on her back and gasps for air and bursts out
crying. Jane and Sally hold her and together they all hug.

Later, they descend into the forest and set up their tents
for the night. At 2am, a flash of lightning cracks across the
sky above and a sudden wind and rain pushes hard like
a hand pressing down to flatten their tents.

Jane screams as her hair gets caught in her sleeping bag's zip. Sally is outside grasping her tent but is showered with leaves and twigs and Sarah stays inside her tent. The storm passes.

Daylight breaks with clear blue skies and warm air. Jane's stomach is screwed up tight with hunger. Her vision blurs and she wobbles for a second as she stands up. Sally is massaging her feet and Sarah's tent is unzipped and open.

'Sarah! Are you there?' says Sally.

No reply. Sally stands up and looks around the campsite and back at Jane.

'Where is she?'

'Perhaps she's gone for a walk?'

'Yes, let's hope so. We must wait, we have time.'

'Yes, I agree.'

Two hours pass and there is no sign of her. They pack up and head for the beach as agreed. Sarah had left her phone in the tent, so the chance of making contact is lost. They head for the boat as planned. The smell of green foliage and soil sticks in the back of Jane's throat and she coughs.

Sally hears the cries, snorting and squawks of chimps and birds up above in the treescape. She slows her steps down and gently moves forward, trying not to break any twigs or draw any attention to them passing underneath. They watch and follow her every step along the treetops. A couple of sticks fall and just miss her head. A roar of laughter erupts from above in the trees and they run off.

They pass an opening and turn to the left. Sally follows closely behind Jane. Left, right, left, right and chop with her knife at the overgrowth blocking their path. It is difficult to see clearly, but the sunlight seeps through and lays out a path.

They pick up a smell of the sea salt air and hear the waves. They break through the last bush and fall onto the white beach. 'Sarah! Sarah! Are you there?' Jane calls, falling to her knees and grabbing the sand. Sally jumps out from behind. 'Sarah!'

There is a rustle from the bushes. Sally runs back into the bushes but there is no one there.

'Sarah! Sarah! We're here!'

No answer. They head for the boat that they tied to a palm tree on the beach when they arrived. They spot a rope but no boat.

'It's gone.'

Jane picks up the rope. She pulls it and out comes a broken bit of wood. 'It was that bloody storm.'

'We're stuck, lost Sarah and no boat.'

'I can't believe it. I can't believe we've lost Sarah.'
'What do you mean, we've lost Sarah? We don't know.
Do we?'
'We should have noticed or heard her.'
'It's not our fault.'
'Isn't it? You wanted to go on this trip. Not me. Just for old
time's sake. The good
times, before we get old.'

'What? Listen. We need to hang on here and find Sarah.'
'Yes, but how?'
'I don't know, we best just wait here as we agreed?'
'Ok, Ok. Yes, let's wait.'
Sally falls to the ground and Jane holds her arm. 'I didn't
want this.'

It was getting dark. They find some fruit trees and pick
some bananas to eat, drink some coconut milk and
wait. The night is cool. They set up their tents, but they
don't sleep.

Day breaks and they heat up some coffee from a can.

They see a tall woman walk towards them from the forest.
She begs them to follow her. She points with her stick to
a small cluster of bushes. They move closer and see Sarah
asleep.

Fruit Machines

Martin Russo

On my commute
I flick my finger
Like a lever.
And up they land
On my screen
Entering my mini-micro world.

One, two, three,
hearts, as I
post an image
Of my last treat;
a strawberry sorbet,
paired with my sparkling spritz.

At my desk,
I flick my finger
Like a lever
and add another post
Into the ring, like throwing dice,
For a chance for another
Heart, like, or thumbs up.

This time, my friends and I are
smiling at a meal. And yes,
That gets me another
six thumbs up from
Julie, Sarah, Susan,
Paul, Jake and Tom.

At the bar,
I flick my finger
Like a lever
after I post a series of images;
a friend of a friend's birthday celebration;
a strawberry shortcake;
sprinkled with a sugary dust.

A group wave hello from a restaurant meal;
Another friend's party snap;
And another snap of a new dish
from a sushi bar.
And yes, that gets me more
Floods of hearts, a thumbs up
and a hundred more likes.

On the train home,
I flick my finger
Like a lever
and watch each new post,
one after the other,
pop, after pop,
going off like a cracker.

In my room
I flick again,
Like a lever
And another hundred likes.
Behind each post,
Hides a story,
And in an instant, a memory flashes past.

One following the next,
like daisy chains,
In close succession,
falling on my page
like drops of rain on my screen.
All aiming, all grabbing
All wanting a microsecond
of my time.

A smile, heart or a like.
So many to see.
Now past midnight,
I flick, flick and flick
Again, with my fat thumb,
Can I stop it?
I don't know.

I just keep going, waiting for
something bright to happen.
Something nice, something light
from the screen, just waiting
for the next like, heart and thumb
and I am one step closer
to the next jackpot.

Review of Dorothea Tanning (1910 - 2012), Tate Modern 27th April 2019.

Martin Russo

I really enjoyed this exhibition and I was struck by the volume of original work pouring out of this new retrospective of Dorothea Tanning's work.

Two decades after Surrealism was born in 1922 and just before Abstract Expressionism art took off in the city, she arrived as an artist in 1940s New York. You would have thought Surrealism by then was a bit old hat, but not for her. It matched her flair for the odd and strange narratives of her works. This was similar to other Surrealists, Salvador Dali and Max Ernst, the latter who later became her husband.

Max Ernst was twenty years her senior. I am not sure how much of his work and art influenced her own. But for me she had her own distinct voice and confidence. She came late to Surrealism while he was one of the early adopters, but both had found inspiration from it.

She said it was good to plumb our deepest subconscious. This fits her odd play on domestic family life: images of doors opening up other worlds, dogs playing, self-portraits and children featuring as her subjects.

Room 1: Birthday (1942) We have the painting that launched her onto the art scene. A self-portrait with ghostly grey pale skin, opened top, a tree like dress, a sitting flying monkey and many doors opening within a door, a key symbol of entering another portal in Surrealism. It strikes me as quite cold and heartless in a way but brilliantly imagined and executed. A real talent.

Room 2: Behind the Door (1984) The canvas is split by a cut off edge of a door in the middle. Perhaps offering another dimension for us? The painting has two girls responding differently to the door painted and stuck on the canvas, with a bright yellow background.

Room 3: The Family Table (1950s) Other paintings here mix green leaves for hair, a big sunflower standing in a hall-way with children, floral colours adorning a girl's clothes, a ghostly father figure over a table and clocks and doors acting as symbolic motifs, throughout. It's not always clear what they mean so does offer some challenges. But per-haps that doesn't matter? They all mix familiar subjects in a new and odd dreamlike fashion.

Room 4: Two Worlds (1950s) We see softer brush strokes and a more 'prismatic' abstract style of painting. She 'began to long for letting it have more freedom.' This could be a sign of her confidence in her work, a move away from her surrealist signs, leaving more space to be relaxed and explore natural responses to her subjects in the paintings.

I was surprised not to see any of her poetry. She was an accomplished award-winning poet later in life. This could have added another layer of her depth and range as an artist; something overlooked perhaps?

Room 7: Hotel Du Pavot Chambre 202 (1970-3) This is a domestic living room with a surrealist twist using soft fabric sculptures of abstracted legs and arms poking out of the walls. She wanted the wallpaper to 'tear with screams' but yet maintain' an odd banality.' She certainly achieved that. The walls were dark red, the lighting quite subdued and I found it strange, odd and somewhat gothic and haunting. I got the sense that her Surrealist ideas had morphed over from paintings to sculpture and they were still quite disturbing in a way.

We finished off with a documentary film from 1979. An attractive, small and playful personality of her unfolds in a somewhat dated and clumsy late seventies art documentary. She talks about her love of dogs, frequently referenced in her work, and about her early life in Illinois, where her family were immigrants from Sweden.

I came out of the exhibition a different person. I found the range staggering and original. I left with a sense of seeing something quite new, unique and somehow as she intended people to have experienced 'never-seen' before art.

2

Brake Pads
Martin Russo

Particulate matter
Float like clouds.

They shower drops
of micro metal dust
across our skies,
blink, and you will still
miss them.

Indiscriminately, they move,
a million particulate
formations drifting
like rudderless boats
across our cityscapes
in miniature.

Some pass through
our gated lips
unnoticed, unregulated,
and unwarranted.

Sliding deeper and deeper,
into our inner space.

Landing without a trace,
In situ, some picked up
In the hectic flow of blood traffic,
hitch-hiked on the back of a red cell

like a parcel train in transit
delivering goods
to hundreds of body parts.

And there they land
And wait, sit and wait.
Not changing, not moving,
soot like dust.
Stuck like pebbles in tissue.

Slowly they leak
wastage, synthetic compounds that so
slightly alters,
so slowly reduces,
our health.

Are you aware of this?
Does pushing the down on another type of pedal not
help?
Is this not something we should stop?
Can we not put the brakes on the brake pads?

Nitrate Dioxide
Martin Russo

Baked in the air,
a copper brown orange
gas that lays like blankets
and moves like herring
in shoals across our city and landscapes.

And if it lived in the sea
it would be spotted
like a drop of red dye
colouring the clear water.

But it doesn't.
Unhinged and invisible, it hovers
Like a hawk, across our paths.

Inhaled it into our lungs
unbeholden of its toxicity.

Now we learn of stunted
growth. A squeeze on lung capacity.
A ticking time bomb of disease.

Armed with facts,
their risks remain hidden.
Protected and buried by something.

The causes are sugar coated
by PR machines. Drilled to dig

out the truth and plant fake truths.
Now we learn how
they twist and turn
in our spaces.

Land in our lungs
adding new coughs, wheezes,
and gasps for air.

How much baking of our air
can we take before we choke?

Waiting
Martin Russo

I am contained,
hard, green and strong.
Resistant to change.
Useful? Yes. Helpful? Of course!
But what I offer is strength,
flexibility, a hardened soul
with a smooth, shiny skin.

Light can pass through me.
Indeed, I have been used a thousand
times and still I scrub up as new.

I am not of my past, my creator.
I merely exist in this green
skin. Sometimes I have been filled
up with liquids, often water, mixed
with a gas that fizzles, pops
and crackles.

Normally I can be picked up
in exchange for round metal.

But now I just lay here, buried
amongst a pile. I know not what to call it.

I sit next to a mountain
of tin, soil, different shaped and coloured pieces like me.
Some are hard and some are soft.

A multitude of us, thousands,
probably millions, if not billions.
Now just sitting and lay waiting.
But for what? I don't know.

I was once busy moving around a lot, going to different
places.
Now I just sit here and wait.

Slowly sinking, slowly buried as more
And more of things like me
sit and hang around.

I believe I must have been here for seventy years now.
Nothing has changed really,
only we have grown and got bigger.

There must be a name for this,
but I just lay here and wait for something
to happen. I can't predict when it
will stop and change. Can you?

Slag
Joanne Anderson

'He called me a slag, for going to work. Can you explain this to me?'

The question was asked by my Spanish friend, who had a baby to a Scouse man. She often asked me to explain things about our culture, when words alone could not be translated.

'I don't know what to tell you,' I said. Some Scouse men will call you a slag if you: disagree with them; don't put their needs first; go out with your mates; go to work; don't have their tea on the table; sleep or don't sleep with someone.

My ex-husband called me it once too - for going to work, for being stuck in traffic and unable to get home in time to collect the baby. He was waiting to go to the gym.

'I wish I was a slag. I don't have the time!' I roared back.

I was too busy running a business whilst bringing up his child while his contribution was £30 a week and two hours on a Wednesday night 'babysitting' his own child.

The term 'slag', I was told by my mother around the age of five is used by men to keep women in their place in this patriarchal society. Never, ever call a woman a slag, I was warned. But at that age, all I thought about was Easter eggs and Findus crispy pancakes.

Slag, as a noun, is used historically and commonly known as a description of the scum of a material matter that is worthless or useless. How did this word also become a way to describe a woman who sleeps around casually and freely, or used to describe a woman at all?

It is used by the Sweeny (a macho TV cop show from the 70s), as a term of abuse for a contemptable person, but not aimed at women in particular. I think it's used differently in Liverpool, as the biggest insult a man can give to a woman. I know Scouse men use it as a 'throwaway comment', but the word has a brutal impact that says to the woman you are worthless and promiscuous (even if this is not literal).

Derry Mathews, a boxer from Liverpool was in the press a week before International Women's Day, for saying in a tweet - 'watch how many match slags go the pub today'.

He was talking about how Liverpool women, in his view, take up seats in the pub for the Derby, pretending to follow football whilst looking for a fella and added that they, 'should stay at home doing the cooking, cleaning and ironing, something you are good at.'

He also has form. In 2013 he was arrested and accused of punching a woman in the face, although it appears, he wasn't charged for this.

I was so angry when I read this that it made my blood boil. I looked through his tweets then and saw a picture of a beautiful young girl around three or four dressed as a ballerina. After this, I was just sad - that this poor girl had a father who talked about women like this.

I hope Derry Mathews' baby girl has the good sense to date someone nothing like her father. I hope she never lets anyone get away with calling her a slag.

It would be easy for us to ignore such a comment as a microaggression, for it not to have any impact. Unfortunately for us in this day and age, women are still very much being kept in their place by such words.

As women, we bear the lion's share of childcare and labour in the home.

We are paid less than men despite doing the same jobs. We're are ignored, marginalised and must fight for all our achievements in the workplace and within business.

On top of that we deal with being stereotyped and sexually harassed.

We are criticised for being too fat or too thin, or not pretty enough, and then there's the violence, the misogyny, the up-skirting and my personal bugbear, the mansplaining.

With this level of discrimination and disrespect it is words like 'slag' that affects our confidence and psyche and is a representation of how women are viewed and treated in society.

One of the areas I have worked on in my career is prosecutions for violence against women and girls. I was appalled and horrified to learn that when England play, whether they win or lose, violence against women incidents go through the roof. Verbal abuse is one of the red flags in terms of domestic violence that starts with the likes of being called a slag.

In England and Wales two women each week are killed by a current or former partner and less than a third of young men prosecuted for rape are convicted.

These disgusting statistics are a reality for women in modern day Britain.

So, Scouse men, I would like you to hear me when I say: complain, disagree and moan, by all means, but when you call a woman a slag – you're saying that they are rubbish and useless and that they're worth less you.

Think about the women in your life and be aware of the impact that word has and how it contributes overall with a drip, drip-like effect, to discrimination and violence experienced by women, every day, everywhere.

A Black British Woman's take on Arthur Jafa's Black America: the good, the bad and the very, very ugly.

Joanne Anderson

As part of the Writing on the Wall's Write for Work pro-gramme, we were asked to review Arthur Jafa's, 'Love is the Message, The Message is Death' at the Tate Liverpool. Typically, I left it until the last minute – two hours before the class – and ran into the Tate from the teeming rain.

The room was vast and pitch black except for the huge screen. The black and white images flicking quickly past overwhelmed me visually like a flipbook animation. The few bodies around me looked like lumps of clothes, bags, and umbrellas without faces.

As soon as an image received recognition in my brain, the video had moved onto the next at a rapid pace. I could hear the preach-like voice of Kayne West singing something about God, but I could not hear the words. I had to filter out what was being said in order to focus on the images bombarding my senses.

I found the quickness of the images similar to how we receive information today at lighting speed, barely able to process the information we receive before moving on. I had entered someway into the seven-minute video of *Black American Imagery* but quickly concluded that the video showed the good, the bad and the very, very ugly aspects of what it is to be Black and American. I stayed to watch it again from the beginning.

The good: I never tire of looking at images of beautiful black people. How can people be racist in the face of so much beauty? Our sheroes and heroes: Nina Simone, Angela Davis, Aretha Franklin, Lauren Hill, Barrack Obama, Malcolm X, Martin Luther, Jimi Hendrix, and the list goes on.

My mother instilled in me from an early age that there is more to black people than sports or music. I am not a sports person and not overly impressed by athletic achievements, nevertheless, sports stars were represented too: basketball players whose names I don't know and Serena Williams celebrating a victory with a 'Crip Walk' (an L.A. street gang dance move).

The civil rights movement and black activism flashed on screen and those images have always been very positive and uplifting for me growing up, something to be immensely proud of. We were taught in British schools that Africans lived in mud huts, captured and enslaved and we were never taught about them fighting back. The Civil Rights movement was empowering; it made me believe that black people could stand up and be listened to, that we could organise and take action.

There was both a cementing and dispelling of stereotypes in this piece of art. I especially liked the image of the black cowboy. I was fascinated when I first saw one on a reality TV show years before. I thought about it for ages and concluded, of course – why wouldn't there be black cowboys, but they were never represented on the American TV shows I watched. My only recollection was Cleavon Little in *Blazing Saddles*, which was satire.

The bad: the over-sexualized images of black women bumping and grinding, something that has always disturbed me. As a black British woman growing up in 70s and 80s England, the only images on TV and film I saw of black women were of prostitutes. When I started dating, I felt like that's what some white man saw when they looked at me.

White people have copied this culture of big lips, hoop earrings and big arses that historically only belonged to black women. I am fascinated by how twerking became a thing after Miley Cyrus did it at the Video Music Awards in 2013. Twerking is said to have originated from the hip-hop movement in New Orleans in the 1980s and was always a black thing. Why does America love black culture but not black people?

Another downside for me was the happy, clappy, church going folks that whip themselves into a frenzy in God's name. Black women are the most religious people in the US. As an atheist-leaning agnostic I have never understood this level of devotion. I hear black people around the world talk about 'God's Will' and 'God's Way'. I don't know whether I envy or respect this blind faith.

There were also images that reminded me of *The Black and White Minstrel Show*. In England, for twenty years on prime-time TV, that lasted up until the late 70s, the BBC aired a programme of white people with blacked up faces.

They pranced about with shiny make-up (like boot polish) faces with big broad ridiculously white smiles portraying some sort of inhuman animal or toy. It wasn't just offensive, it hurt that this show was so popular with sixteen million viewers.

The very, very ugly: the violence, injustice, abuse, discrimination, police brutality, the having to fight for your civil rights, the necessity of the Black Lives Matter movement and the Ku Klux Klan.

A young black boy confused as to why his father was telling him to put his hands up. I too was taught by my mother about being stopped by the police, told to 'never answer back', the talk, I have also had with my son.

It is painful to recall the image of a black boy being arrested, crying, 'I want my mom.' I never want to see another image of a black person being beaten or murdered at the hands of the police.

The artwork may have been about Black America, but I identified with every image as just 'black'. When something happens to one black person, it happens to us all. Many think the Black Lives Matter movement and deaths of black people at the hands of police is something that only happens in America. I have learned in-depth, that it happens here too. The figures of black people dying in police custody without consequences in the UK make for shocking reading; the difference is they rarely shoot them down in the street.

As a Race Equality professional for nearly thirty years I feel like the world has moved backward with all the rhetoric and negative dialogue about black people that has arisen from the likes of Trump and Brexit supporters. A key example is Nigel Farage saying that black men are more violent due to a higher rate of testosterone. How impudent with the history of violence against black people, the violence of colonialism, apartheid, the violent brutality of white supremacy and economic oppression. What's a white man's excuse for their violent acts?

You may think by all my complaining and negativity about this piece of art that I didn't like it. The opposite is true. It is naked and raw and provides an excellent display of how the black community is glorified, fetishised, demonised and traumatised.

If art is meant to make you look a little bit closer at social issues, at other people and the issues that surround them, then this piece well and truly does its job. It moved me; it made me cry. Feedback from my fellow writers tell me I wasn't alone in my tears.

At the exhibition as soon as the lights came on, people couldn't wait to get out of the room. They were almost running. I wish I could run away from this, but I can't. I'm black. This is what we must deal with and the artwork shows it in all its beauty, pain and terror.

Arthur Jafa says about his work, that in everything he does, 'I never speak to white people, I always speak to black people.' As black people we already know, we live it. I hope this work does speak to white people; I hope it inspires them, as it does me – to be an active anti-racist in this messed up racist world.

Danielle
Joanne Anderson

'Whatever, I'm easy,' was Danielle's answer to almost any question asked.

Danielle and I, friends since primary school, had very different personalities.

But we were always getting into trouble in school. Danielle, blonde, blue-eyed and petite, never getting the punishment, smiling and angelic looking. I, on the other hand, 6ft, black-skinned, sturdy and would argue back with teachers by moaning and groaning, making my fate worse.

I discovered she was dating an older guy when I saw this greasy-haired, scrawny looking fella with rat-like features drag her like a rag doll into his car as we left school.

'What was that about?' I asked the next day.

'I was late. I've been seeing him for a couple of months. He didn't want me to tell anyone because he is older than me, people won't understand,' she said defensively.

'Urgh he's horrible, Danielle,' I said. 'A man dragging you into a car and telling you to keep the relationship on the down-low from your friends sounds abusive to me.'

When she fell pregnant at fourteen, I'm sure Danielle's mum blamed me, the loud-mouthed trouble causer. But it wasn't my fault. I kept most men very much at arm's length. After school, we had stayed in touch infrequently. I moved away to work at a holiday camp working seventeen-hour days, while the remaining hours were filled with drinking, partying and good times. I imagined that Danielle was left holding the baby, trapped at home night after night, while soft lad did whatever he wanted, her saying nothing.

When I returned home, I arrived in my banged up yellow Volkswagen Beetle. Danielle was really impressed that I had a car at twenty.

'I've done nothing with my life,' she complained.

'Don't be daft, Danielle, look at this beautiful little prince you have,' I said, tickling baby Michael to the sound of raucous chuckles.

I hadn't seen Danielle for a while when I got a call out of the blue.

'Can you pick me up from the hospital? I've just had another baby and I need a lift home.'

I was shocked again she hadn't informed me of her news.

'Of course, but where is their dad?' I asked.

He hadn't shown; what a deadbeat. He wasn't even there for the birth. I couldn't believe that she had stayed with this loser for nearly a decade. I had heard horrible things about him, including drug dealing and armed robberies,

stories Danielle seemed to know nothing about.
The baby, another beautiful boy, was a tiny little thing
dressed up in blue with that new baby smell. Perfect in
every way, except for a yellowing tinge on his skin.

'Danielle, does the baby look like he has jaundice to you?'
I queried. 'Why don't I ask the doctors about it, better to
ask now than worry when you get home.'

Danielle, of course, nodded agreement.

I moved out into the busy corridor and saw a handsome
doctor in a white coat looking pensively up at a white
board filled with patient information.

'Doctor, do you mind having a look at the baby – does he
look like he has jaundice to you?'

'Hmmm, let's have a look,' he said in a posh accent. Looking uneasy, he took a hold of the baby and informed us
that he would be right back. Danielle continued packing
her stuff ready to go home and was in good form, laughing
and chatting. She appeared unconcerned.

A nurse peered around the corner. 'Come on then, Danielle,
let's get you signed out ready for home,' she said warmly.
She asked where the baby was. We explained that the
doctor had taken him to see if he had jaundice. She asked
what the doctor's name was. We didn't know, but gave a
description of a tall blonde haired, blue-eyed and softly
spoken man.

The nurse came back fifteen minutes later, in a visible fluster. 'We have no doctor here of that description, Danielle. We can't find your baby.'

Danielle cried out like a wounded animal and it felt like someone had punched me in the stomach, knocking out every breath.

The hospital was locked down. Security guards were checking everyone, and police interviews were taking place. I couldn't shake the feeling that the father was behind this, and I was determined to find out why.

Letter to a Nurse just Starting Out
Karen Woolrich

Dear Nursing Colleague,

May I take this opportunity to congratulate you on qualifying as a nurse. It hasn't been an easy journey and has tested you to the limit. However, you have chosen a profession which I can only describe as the best job in the world. You have chosen a profession where you will be constantly learning and challenging yourself. You could be having the worst day in the world but on reflection you will have had the best day when your patient starts to make progress. This will because despite the outcome you know you have done your best, worked hard as a team and done everything possible to care for your patients. There are no two days the same; routine is so boring and overrated anyway. You have the privilege to meet and care for new patients and their families. You will meet new staff, both nursing and medical. You will work, learn and support each other together. You are a nurse now, but will soon become a counsellor, a teacher and a mentor. You will pick up skills you didn't even know you had, until you need to use them.

I would like to introduce myself to you. I qualified late in life as a staff nurse at the age of forty. It was a profession I had always wanted to do from a young age but left school with limited qualifications. While my children were young, I completed an Access to Higher Education science course, but didn't use it until the time my eldest child went to

secondary school. In the meantime, I worked as an aux-
iliary nurse for seventeen years at the Royal Liverpool
University Hospital on a mixed surgical unit. There were
a few reasons why I didn't start training to be a nurse as
soon as I passed the access to Higher Education course.
The main reason was that I was unable to afford to train.
The nursing bursary was too low to justify training with
a young family to feed and clothe. However, thanks to a
Labour government the bursary increased and covered my
part-time wages. With only one child to take to school and
make arrangements for I was encouraged and supported
by my friends to apply and to start nurse training. They
promised that between them they would help me take
and pick up my boy from school. Big shout out to Lesley
and Julie; without your help qualifying would not have
been possible.

I am coming into my twelfth year as a qualified intensive
care nurse. I absolutely love my job and have met the most
amazing patients and their families. I have met people
who have been through the worst pain imaginable but
have also been the bravest and most dignified people I
will ever meet. They teach you lessons that you will use
in your own life. They teach you to live life to the full.
When you think you're having a bad day, on reflection,
you're really not. They teach you to be resilient, kind and
appreciate the little things in life. They teach you to look
after your parents because you won't have them forever.

Working in the NHS I have seen it many times at its
absolute best and it makes me proud each day I have the
privilege to work in it. That is why I'm prepared to fight

for it as long I have the energy and strength to do so. But I can't fight alone; I need your help. I continue to write this letter feeling tearful and emotional because the NHS I love so much will be unrecognisable in a few years' time. This most precious organisation which was built after the sacrifice and devastation left after the Second World War is about to be dismantled and privatised and it is our public duty as nurses, as our patients' advocates to raise awareness.

Our amazing NHS is something that has evolved and grown. Research has played a major role in developing pathways saving lives and improving health outcomes immensely. There is so much potential for further improvements: to invest in research for cancer treatment, treatment for dementia, treatment to improve neonatal deaths and stillbirths, to fight against sepsis. There is so much potential to improve what the NHS can offer. What kind of country do we live in that denies children lifesaving treatment? What kind of society do we live in when health outcomes are determined by which part of the country we live in? What kind of country do we live in when expectant mothers are being turned away from maternity units? What kind of country do we live in when we can't look after our senior citizens with the dignity and love they deserve? What kind of country do we live in when this government is determined to privatise services section by section under our noses?

Health services are not effective if costs are cut and safety compromised. How is it we are in the position now that diagnostic services have been tendered out to the private sector? I can give you many examples of NHS services that have been placed into private hands and have failed and been brought back into the NHS, but they are too numerous to mention.

Health economics is an interesting subject. I won't keep you too much longer, but I would like you to consider this. Don't listen if anyone says to you as a country that we need to live within our means and can't afford an NHS that is free at the point of need, paid for by general taxation and publicly provided. A comprehensive and a universal service for all is possible. We are the sixth richest country in the world. It's about how wealth and income are redistributed. Consider the vast profits made by pharmaceutical companies, charging governments extortionate amounts for drugs. Nationalise the pharmaceutical industry and reinvest the profits for further research. Stop spending ludicrous amount of money in agency fees and employ more NHS nurses. Reduce health inequalities and there will be fewer sick days and loss of earnings. Stop giving compensation to multination companies for loss of contracts being awarded; the list is endless. I will leave it there, but I hope I have given you food for thought. I know you are busy and probably tired like me so I will leave you with one final message: if you are not already in a union, please join one today. Join the fight to save the NHS and keep up the good work.

About the Writers

Debra Chisango

Debra Chisango is an aspiring writer who gives credit to WoW for the opportunity. She was born in Zimbabwe and is a qualified chef and desires to see people realise that food is a gift from God and not take it for granted. Debra believes that writing is a way of expressing the inner thoughts and feelings that one can't say. Her passion is to see African women find their voices and speak up on abuse whether physically, mentally or emotionally. She is a Christian and her life's journey is routed on Jeremiah 29:11-14.

Nina T

Nina T was born in Liverpool and is a graduate of the Surrey Institute of Art and Design with a BA (Hons) in Animation. After an eighteen -year career detour via the rock 'n' roll world of finance, the heady thrill of numbers is wearing thin and she is back on the creative writing road. A keen storyteller, she has often been told, 'You need to write this stuff down!' so the plan is to do just that. As a physically disabled social butterfly, she has a unique insight into the 'joys' of being 'different' in the real world which is often reflected in her work - the aim being to disarm with humour, sucker punch with reality!

E-mail: NINATHOMSON@sky.com
Twitter: @MissyNT

Nicki McCubbing

Nicki McCubbing was born in 1977 and lives in Liverpool. Nicki studied Fine Art and has worked as a sculptor and installation artist since 1999, exhibiting her work both nationally and internationally. Since having children, Nicki has been developing the creative writing she has done privately for many years. Writing on the Wall has given her the opportunity to learn new writing skills to finish the script she has in development. The story is the uncanny plight of a teenage girl in 1991 who starts her period the moment Freddie Mercury dies.

Anthony McCarthy

Anthony McCarthy was born in Liverpool. At school, he was a member of the football team. He did a few other sports. Anthony always had an interest in literature. He went to university and got a degree in French and Italian. And he went back to higher education, got a PGCE, and became a secondary school teacher of languages. Anthony now does some language teaching for the WEA and volunteers to teach English to asylum seekers in Liverpool. He also volunteers in FACT as a gallery assistant. His main interests are literary reviews and short stories.

Mitty Ramagavigan

Mitty Ramagavigan had worked in the cultural sector for close to a decade and is keen to explore and inform the past, present and future of Liverpool. In her limited spare time, she enjoys cooking, hanging out with her friends and family and watching too much *RuPaul's Drag Race*. She heard about the WoW course by chance and signed up as the opportunity was too good to miss. 'I can't believe how much I've learnt over these past few months, it's been such an incredible experience and I really enjoyed getting to meet the others in the featured anthology.' The course has inspired her to start a blog called Life in Colour, exploring art made and featuring women of colour which she'll be launching in autumn, if she doesn't chicken out!

Natalie Reeves-Billing

Natalie has always found biographies terribly hard to write. So definite. So factual. Absolutely no space to embellish or polish. But, the essence of her can be summed up in a few words: music, words, creativity, randomness and disorder. She knew that the conventional route wasn't going to be hers. Natalie tried a bit of everything. When the kids came along, she found a new love for children's stories. Natalie started to write them down and use her children as test subjects. Now, she's developing a children's TV and book range titled *The Bubs*, alongside penning her first young adult novel.

Karen Bryony Rose

Karen has been writing ever since she was old enough to hold a pen. Her short fiction has appeared in magazines, Girl Gang Zine and Dear Damsels. She also writes non-fiction, on topics ranging from mental health to psychological abuse. She's been volunteer editor for several local charities and is now a custodian of history and knowledge by profession. Drawn to the darker side of human nature, she loves the gothic and has an interest in psychology, history and nature. She does her best writing by the sea.

Find her on Twitter: @SunSparks4
Web: https://wordpress.com/view/thequietplace.video.blog

Vicky M Andrews

Vicky M Andrews is a freelance content writer and author of the blog 'Planet Vicster - An Introvert's Guide to the Galaxy'. She has bounced back from redundancy three times and prefers being her own boss now because, she says, 'It's much harder to get sacked.' Vicky is a regular food and drink contributor at Liverpool Confidential and her punchy reviews have been described as, 'hilarious and brilliant [with] an excellent gift for writing.'

Martin Russo

Martin Russo is a published writer of flash fiction and short stories. He also writes poetry and is working towards developing and completing a novel. He has always enjoyed writing since he was young and has continued to develop creative writing since graduating with a degree in English and later a master's degree in journalism, which included an option studying screenwriting. He aims to combine his writing and journalistic skills in developing a digital media platform in his local community supporting local arts, along with some local investigative news stories.

Joanne Anderson

Born and bred in Liverpool, Joanne is passionate about tackling social injustice. Joanne's profession is business consultancy and she has nearly thirty years' experience of supporting organisations from a range of sectors in achieving equality and inclusion outcomes. Joanne lives with her sixteen-year-old son who is an artist and all round bright young thing. Joanne would never describe herself as creative but is an avid reader and lover of the arts. Gobby by nature, the Writing on the Wall, Write for Work course has allowed Joanne to express herself in a way she never thought she could.

For further updates on the story 'Danielle', please contact: anderson-joanne@sky.com

Karen Woolrich

Karen Woolrich was born in Oldham, Lancashire. She moved to Liverpool in 1989. Karen studied at the University of Central Lancashire. She is married with two children, and loves cooking, gardening, live music and theatre. Karen is also part of the Save the Liverpool Women's Hospital Campaign.

WOW WRITING ON THE WALL

Congratulations to all those who participated in Write For Work for producing such quality writing and being generous enough to share their stories with us.

Writing on the Wall is a dynamic, Liverpool-based community organisation that celebrates writing in all its forms. We hold an annual festival and a series of year-round projects. We work with a broad and inclusive definition of writing that embraces literature, creative writing, journalism and nonfiction, poetry, song-writing, and storytelling. We work with local, national and international writers whose work provokes controversy and debate, and with all of Liverpool's communities to promote and celebrate individual and collective creativity. WoW's creative writing projects support health, wellbeing and personal development.

If you have a story to tell, or would like to take part in, or work with WoW to develop a writing project, please get in touch – we'd love to hear from you.

Mike Morris and Madeline Heneghan, Co-Directors

info@writingonthewall.org.uk
www.writingonthewall.org.uk
0151 703 0020
@wowfest